CHAMPAK

Started in 1969, Champak is the largest-selling children's magazine in India. Published in eight languages and reaching over six million kids, it's an inseparable part of childhood memories for most Indians. Champak's stories are beautifully illustrated, expand creativity and imagination, hone reading skills and bring positive self-worth. Through its stories, Champak encourages children to treat others with respect, kindness and sensitivity, helps develop cognitive and reasoning skills, and brings humour that is essential to a child's everyday life.

Published by
Rupa Publications India Pvt. Ltd 2025
7/16, Ansari Road, Daryaganj
New Delhi 110002

Sales centres:
Bengaluru Chennai
Hyderabad Jaipur Kathmandu
Kolkata Mumbai Prayagraj

Copyright © Delhi Press Patra Prakashan Pvt. Ltd., 2025

This is a work of fiction. Names, characters, places and incidents are either the product of the authors' imagination or are used fictitiously and any resemblance to any actual person, living or dead, events or locales is entirely coincidental.

All rights reserved.
No part of this publication may be reproduced, transmitted, or stored in a retrieval system, in any form or by any means, electronic, mechanical, photocopying, recording or otherwise, without the prior permission of the publisher.

P-ISBN: 978-93-6156-342-3
E-ISBN: 978-93-6156-278-5

First impression 2025

10 9 8 7 6 5 4 3 2 1

Printed in India

This book is sold subject to the condition that it shall not, by way of trade or otherwise, be lent, resold, hired out, or otherwise circulated, without the publisher's prior consent, in any form of binding or cover other than that in which it is published.

CHAMPAK
SCHOOL DAY
STORIES

RUPA

To the years we spend in school...

Table of Contents

RED-NOSED RITWIK	5
BACK TO SCHOOL	9
ANITA'S SPECIAL ANNUAL DAY	16
TEACHERS, POOR CREATURES!	20
THE AWARD	26
RAIN OF STARS!	32
HESITATION NO MORE	37
AND THEY BECAME FRIENDS	42
SHANTANU'S WILD ADVENTURE	47
ACHOO!	50
A LESSON IN EQUALITY	55
WE ARE EQUAL	59
SEEMA FINDS HER CONFIDENCE	65
CHEATING THE TEACHER	71

JUMPY'S PRIDE	74
BLINDED BY PRIDE	79
IN A NEW CITY	83
ISHA'S FIRST DAY	88
MITTU GOES TO SCHOOL	95
THE WRONG KIND OF HELP	98
A PIECE OF PAPER	103
THE FOREST ECHOES WITH NEWS	108
MY DEAREST TEACHERS	114
A BOX OF CHOCOLATES	119
FIRST DAY AT SCHOOL	127

Self-Discovery

Friendship

Teamwork

Humour

Learning

Red-Nosed Ritwik

By Rahul Bhandare

Ritwik boarded the school bus, BRIMMING with excitement. His family had just moved to Hyderabad and the thought of a new school and new friends excited him.

Ritwik looked around the bus and **SMILED** at the new faces. The other children smiled back at him.

After some time, the bus reached the school. A wide-eyed Ritwik was guided by his new friends to his classroom. The SIZE of the class came as a surprise to him. Back in Jaipur, where his previous school was, there were just 30 students in a class. Here, there were around 60!

Ritwik began to feel slightly NERVOUS. He found a seat at the back of the class.

A boy was sitting behind Ritwik who kept glaring at him. Even when Ritwik smiled, the boy continued to glare at him.

A girl sitting next to Ritwik whispered to him, "Hey, don't look at him. Jatin seems to be in a BAD mood today. We all avoid talking to him on such days."

At that moment, their class teacher entered the class and

began taking attendance. When he reached Ritwik's name, he paused.

"Oh yes! Class, we have a **new** student with us," announced Swapnil sir. "Please come here, Ritwik."

A Nervous Introduction

As Ritwik stood up and walked, he felt the eyes of 60-odd children on him. Swapnil sir stood beside him and said, "Ritwik,

tell the class a little bit about yourself."

"My name is Ritwik Prabhakar," Ritwik began nervously. "I'm from Jaipur. My father works in a car company. Umm…I like to play **cricket**…"

As Ritwik was speaking, the school attendant came in and handed a note to the teacher. After reading the note, Swapnil sir excused himself and went out. Ritwik stood there, unsure whether to continue speaking or go back to his seat. For a few seconds, the whole class was **SILENT**. Ritwik cleared his throat and continued, "I… umm… like to bat and bowl."

"Is that so? And how good are you at **fielding**?" shouted Jatin, who then threw an eraser at Ritwik. Before Ritwik could react, the eraser hit him hard on his nose. The entire class burst into loud fits of **l·ughter**. Ritwik realised that his nose had turned a bright red.

Name-Calling

Jatin started to sing, "Ritwik, the tomato-nosed boy, has a very shiny nose! Red-nosed Ritwik! Red-nosed Ritwik!"

Soon, all the students repeated the CHANT. With tears in his eyes, Ritwik ran out of the class. He had only run a few steps when he bumped into Swapnil Sir.

"Ritwik! What happened?" asked his teacher with concern.

He narrated the entire incident to Swapnil sir.

After hearing Ritwik's story, Swapnil sir said, "There's something I'd like to show you, Ritwik. Come with me."

A Lesson From The Teacher

After walking through a couple of corridors, Ritwik found himself standing in front of a table that had some old books on it. The teacher took out an old YEARBOOK from the pile and opened it.

"I too, studied at his school. Do you see that boy in the first row? That was me!" said the teacher, pointing at a class photograph.

Ritwik looked at the picture. The boy his teacher pointed to looked small and timid.

"When I moved to this school, the nickname I got was Shorty; this stuck with me all through school."

Ritwik was surprised. He looked at his teacher and let out a chuckle. His teacher was around SIX-FEET TALL! To think of teasing him about his height seemed silly. But it all made sense to Ritwik now.

The teacher smiled and said, "I'll give you a five-minute head start. Get to the class before me, young man."

Ritwik Bounces Back

Ritwik wiped his tears and ran back to the class. As he entered, the whole class ERUPTED in a loud chant again: "Red-nosed Ritwik! RED-NOSED RITWIK!"

Ritwik threw a small piece of CHALK up in the air and hit it with his NOSE. Seeing this, everyone laughed and so did Ritwik. Jatin was now again in a bad mood. He quietly sat down on the last bench. On the other hand, red-nosed Ritwik was feeling much better. He settled down in his seat with a big smile on his face.

Back to School

By Sudha Vijay

"Nitya! I have some good **NEWS** for you," called out Nitya's mother. "Your Dad just told me that you'll be joining one of the best schools in this city. Tomorrow will be your **FIRST** day."

"Okay, Mom," said 10-year-old Nitya. She was not **excited**. She silently went to her room, closed the door and sat on the bed, thinking of her old school and friends.

Nervous Nitya

Nitya had lived in Chennai all her life. But her father's transfer brought their family to Delhi.

Why did we move to this city? All my friends are in Chennai. I won't have any friends in this school. I can't even speak Hindi **FLUENTLY**. *I wish I could have stayed at my friend Tara's house,* she thought.

Nitya remembered her old life. She loved going to school in **Chennai**. She loved meeting her friends and taking part in dance competitions. In this city, she had no reason to look forward to going to school.

I'll be joining in the middle of the year. It will be

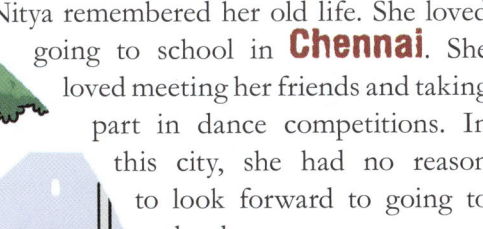

DIFFICULT *to make new friends. And everyone will stare at me when I go to class*, she worried.

Feeling **low**, she packed her school bag and gathered her things, and she remained sad the rest of the day.

In the evening, when Nitya's father came back home, he gave her a big **hug** and a bar of chocolate. "Nitya, you must always be ready to face **CHALLENGES**. I know that you're upset because we moved to this city, but remember that people are the same everywhere. If you talk to them nicely, they'll be nice to you, too," he said.

"Moreover, you are a friendly person. I'm sure you'll make **FRIENDS** quickly," added Mom.

Nitya simply nodded her head. That night she was unable to sleep. She **tossed** and turned in bed, dreading the day ahead.

The Dreadful First Day

The next morning, Nitya's school bus picked her up at seven o'clock and dropped her off near the main entrance of the school. Nitya found her way to the classroom.

Nitya took a deep breath and entered the class. Everyone turned around to look at her. She became **nervous** as she was being stared at by her classmates. As she walked past them, she heard a lot of murmurs.

"Look, her **HAIR** is so long," said a boy who was sitting in the front row.

"Is she good at **STUDIES**?" asked another.

Nitya quietly sat in a back-row seat. To her relief, a teacher walked in. After attendance, Nitya was introduced to the whole class.

"Students, meet your new classmate, Nitya Nagarajan. She is good at studies and is also a CLASSICAL dancer. I hope that everyone makes her feel welcome," said the teacher.

Nitya waved at her class and returned to her seat.

A short-haired girl sitting beside her shook Nitya's hand and said, "Hi, my name is Ritu. Nice to meet you. I, too, love dancing."

At the start of every class, Ritu told Nitya a little about the teacher who was teaching that subject. The morning passed quickly and before Nitya knew it, it was lunchtime.

Ritu said, "Nitya, why don't you join me and my friends for LUNCH?"

Nitya politely refused. Ritu and her friends sat in a circle and shared their lunchboxes with one another.

Nitya unzipped her bag to take out her lunch box but realised that she'd left it on her study table at home. Nitya's stomach was growling with hunger, but she did not have money to buy anything from the school canteen. She closed her eyes and laid her head down on her desk.

Sharing Lunch And Laughter

After a moment, Nitya felt somebody's hand on her **shoulders**. She turned around and found Ritu looking at her with concern.

"Are you feeling **sick**?" asked Ritu.

"Not really. It's just a headache," replied Nitya.

"Hunger will make your headache worse. My mother has made some **aloo parathas**. Would you like to taste them?" asked Ritu, brightly.

Nitya simply could not say no. She ate a small part of the paratha.

"Thank you. The parathas are really **delicious**," said Nitya.

"What did you bring for lunch? Won't you share your lunchbox with us?" asked another classmate.

Nitya said sadly, "Actually, I **forgot** to bring my lunch today."

"Oh. Why didn't you tell us before?" asked Ritu.

Soon, Nitya was surrounded by her new classmates who **offered** their lunchboxes to her. They asked her about

Chennai, her old school, friends and dance practice. Nitya too chatted away with them.

By the end of the day, Nitya knew the names of most of her classmates. Everyone decided to include her in their play time during the recess hour and also take her help for the upcoming **CULTURAL** festival in school.

Nitya Feels Welcomed

After the last class was over, Ritu said, "Nitya, today we shared our lunchboxes with you. But before we accept you as our friend, you'll have to perform a **special** task."

Nitya was shocked. She asked suspiciously, "What task?"

"You have to bring **SOUTH INDIAN** dishes, like idlis and dosas, for us tomorrow," blurted out Ritu.

The class burst out **LAUGHING** and Nitya happily agreed.

When Nitya reached home, her mother immediately said, "I saw your lunchbox on the study table! Did you eat anything the entire day?"

"Don't worry, Mom. My new friends **shared** their food with me," said Nitya.

"Oh! So, you've already made new friends," said Mom.

In the evening Nitya's father asked her, "So dear, how was your first day at school?"

Nitya replied cheerfully, "It was great, Dad. You were right! This city is full of warm people and I am happy that I got to meet some of them."

Nitya's parents smiled at each other in RELIEF. They were happy to see their daughter smile again.

"Mom, will you pack DOSAS for me and my friends tomorrow? It seems that they love dosas!" Nitya said.

"Of course, I will!" her mother replied.

Solve It

Cheeku is writing a note about his first day of school in his diary. By looking at the panels, complete the passage to guess what he's writing.

1 Today was the first day of _____. I got dressed quickly and ran all the way there, where I met _____ and _____. I climbed up on _____ and checked the list to see if we would all be in the same class.

2 Yes! _____, _____ and I were together. Our first subject was_____, and we went to class.

3 After attendance was taken, our_____ wanted to know what we did during our _____. When it was my turn, I told the _____ how I learned how to _____.

4 After_____, I said bye to my _____ and returned _____.

Anita's Special Annual Day

By Prema Ramakrishnan

One Sunday afternoon, Anita was reading a book at home. She loved to read, especially **POEMS**. She would read them several times until she knew the **VERSES** by heart. This time, as she was reading, she thought of a poem. She quickly typed it on her computer and showed it to her mother.

"That is a lovely poem, Anita! You must share it with your friends. I am sure they will **LOVE** it," said her mother.

Anita's Poem

The next day at school, Anita read out her poem to her best friend, Meera. She also loved it. Anita was thrilled. Later, when her friend Swathi heard her poem, she suggested that they do a **performance** based on the poem for their school's annual day.

So, the three girls asked their class teacher whether they could go ahead with their idea.

"Yes, of course you can. Anita, do you think you can direct the performance since the poem is yours?" asked their class teacher.

"Yes, ma'am. I want to try," replied Anita.

After class, the three of them sat together to plan about the performance.

Performance Preparations

"Since the title of the poem is '**THE SEASONS**', I think it would be nice to have props to go with it," suggested Swathi.

"Exactly! I was thinking we could make five trees to represent the five different seasons. For **SPRING**, we'll make a tree with lots of flowers on it. The **summer** tree will be dry, while the monsoon tree will be bright with green leaves. The **AUTUMN** tree will have brown leaves, and no leaves and only hints of white to show snow for the **winter** tree," explained Anita.

"We will have just one tree at a time on stage. Depending on the season we will be describing in our performance, we will bring that particular tree on stage. We will have to **dim** the lights when we change the setting," she added.

"Great **idea**!" exclaimed Meera. "I will ask my mother to help me record some sounds of *BIRDS* and water and transfer

those on to a CD; the music can be played in the background. We can practise our dance along with it."

Anita and Swathi agreed. The three went to their class teacher and discussed their ideas with her.

And The Work Begins

"That sounds wonderful!" said their teacher. "Anita, you can **RECITE** the poem. I can help you with the stage lights but you have to give me the details of the scenes, so that we can coordinate correctly," she added.

The girls **PLANNED** every detail of their performance carefully and also worked on the **props**. They practised their dance every day after school and even got more students to join in.

Finally, the day of their performance arrived. They waited backstage for their turn. When their names were called out, they stepped on to the **STAGE**.

At first, the stage was dark. As the music began to play, the lights came on and revealed a beautiful tree at the centre of the stage with branches full of BEAUTIFUL flowers. The music slowly faded and Anita began reciting her poem.

A Spectacular Performance

When the lines described summer, the tree changed to **GULMOHAR**. Then came monsoon accompanied by sounds of the rain, thunder and **LIGHTNING**. Autumn's tree appeared with its browns- and yellow-coloured leaves. Finally, it was the quiet winter. Throughout the performance, the dancers moved **gracefully** to the tune of the music.

Their performance received a thunderous **applause**. The girls beamed with joy. Anita was the **HAPPIEST**. A poem written by her had made it all possible!

Teachers, Poor Creatures!

By S. Varalakshmi

Bluebell School was celebrating **Teachers' Day**. The sixth-grade students had volunteered to teach the junior classes. Hari and Laxman, two sixth graders, were talking to each other on their way to the fourth-grade classroom.

"I don't feel I should be **STRICT**. Teachers need to loosen up a bit," said Laxman.

Hari replied, "I agree. The kids are going to love us. I am sure we could make a **CAREER** out of this."

"Easy job, easy money," Laxman said. They both grinned as they entered the classroom.

The classroom was filled with **NOISY** kids. As soon as they saw Hari and Laxman, they started cheering for them. Hari and Laxman grinned at each other.

"Good morning, **friends**. I'm calling you friends because we are going to be like friends with each other today," said Hari.

The children clapped **enthusiastically**.

The First Lesson

Laxman cleared his throat and said, "Okay, friends, take out your **history** books." The children groaned and obeyed.

Hari asked, "Can someone tell me about the history of India? What can India be **PROUD** of?"

A student got up and said, "**Me**! India can be proud of me."

The class burst out laughing.

Laxman asked, "Do you mind telling us what you did to make India proud?"

The student said cheekily, "I poured **ketchup** on Ritesh's head." Again, laughter followed.

Hari murmured to Laxman, "Be patient."

Hari said, "Getting back to the topic, can you tell me about the historical event that took place in Agra?"

Chaos Ensues

Frowning, the boy thought and said, "Of course! **Agra ka petha**! My mom packed some for lunch. Want some?"

Hari gave up and asked Laxman to take over.

Laxman asked the class, "Can someone tell me one good and one bad deed that you did today?"

A girl stood up and said, "I offered a **BREAD** slice to Rohan and the bad deed…Well…"

"Go on," Laxman prodded.

She replied, looking down, "I ate his bag of CHIPS without informing him."

Rohan screamed, "You did what? How could you?"

The kids kept arguing with each other, and Hari and Laxman wondered what they had got themselves into. Still, they decided not to give up.

One More Teaching Atempt

Laxman repeated the question. Then a boy came forward and handed a **gift-wrapped** box to them. Surprised and touched, the boys opened it. Two FROGS leapt out. Both the boys screamed loudly.

Hari shouted, "What is the meaning of this?"

The boy said, "That is my **BAD** deed for today."

Laxman snapped at him, "May I ask what is your good deed for today?"

The boy grinned and answered, "Well, at first, I kept one frog inside but I thought he would get lonely. So, I kept another frog in the box to keep him company. Wasn't that a thoughtful gesture?"

Hari and Laxman were horror-struck. They said angrily, "The class has had enough fun. Now it's time to study seriously. Open your history books."

One of the students said loudly, "Hey, dude! We are not in the mood to study today."

Another student got up and said, "Friend, how about some Rock and Roll?"

A Messy Affair!

Within seconds, there was utter **chaos** in the classroom. Some students were singing loudly, some were **drumming**

at their desks; some were dancing on the benches and some were running around, trying to catch one another.

Suddenly, one of the kids jumped on Hari. He lost his **BALANCE** and fell with a thud. Another kid jumped on Laxman's back and told the class, "I am going to ride on my friend's back today."

Then the kid asked Laxman, "Hey friend, shall I **grab** your neck or your hair?"

The class **cheered** and clapped. Hari and Laxman's clothes were **torn** and their hair became messy. They looked around in horror.

Others started yelling, "I want a ride too."

Seeing students running towards them, Hari and Laxman yelled, "HELP! HELP!"

Thankfully, a teacher who was passing by heard their cries for help and **rescued** them.

Hari and Laxman made their way out of the class **SHEEPISHLY**. They wondered how they ever believed that a teacher's job was easy.

Observe the picture for a minute, cover it and try answering the questions given below.

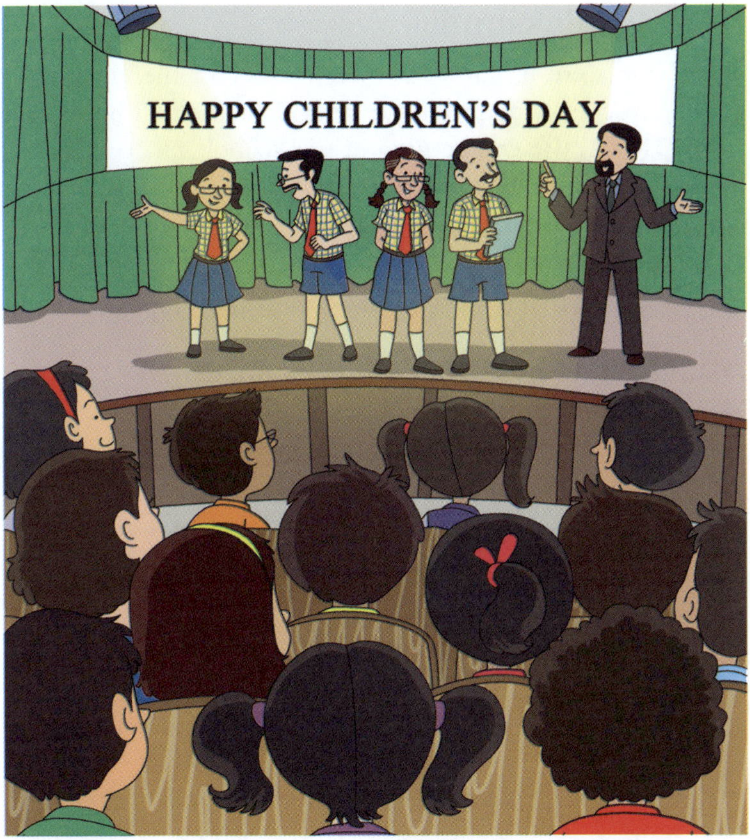

Q1. How many teachers are performing on stage?

Q2. What is the colour of their uniform?

Q3. How many students are sitting in the front row?

Q4. What is written on the banner placed on the stage?

The Award

By S. Varalakshmi

Students were listening to their teacher in the classroom. The teacher announced, "In four days, we will be having a **MONOLOGUE** competition in our school. The participant has to speak on a subject without taking a break or a pause. Our class has to win this **AWARD**, students. Now, tell me who wants to participate in this contest?"

The teacher looked at the students and smiled hopefully.

Mischief Leads To Participation

No one wanted to volunteer. Ritesh nudged his friend Abhay who was sitting next to him. "Shall I give your name?" Ritesh whispered.

Abhay glared and whispered back, "Don't you **DARE**."

Ritesh chuckled and held up his arm in the air. The teacher looked very pleased.

She said, "Excellent, Ritesh. I was hoping someone from my class would **volunteer**."

Ritesh stood up and said hesitatingly, "Uhh... Teacher, not me. Actually, Abhay wants to take part. He is too **shy** to volunteer."

Saying this, Ritesh looked at Abhay's **SHOCKED** expression.

The teacher looked at Abhay and said, "That is wonderful, Abhay. I am **PROUD** of you." Fearfully, Abhay got up and **FALTERED**, "No Ma'am, I… He…"

But the teacher was too busy writing down his name on the paper to listen to him. Poor Abhay had no choice but to sit down. He was angry and also felt **HELPLESS**.

The teacher turned to the rest of the class and asked, "Is anyone else interested? I need one more person."

Ritesh was trying hard to control his **LAUGHTER**, while Abhay saw his opportunity as soon as the teacher said this. Abhay held up his hand and said **LOUDLY**, "Ma'am, Ritesh here would like to give his name." Ritesh had not expected this.

The teacher looked at Ritesh and asked, "Why didn't you say so before, Ritesh?"

Ritesh nervously **BABBLED**, "Ma'am… Abhay here… No… I…can't…"

The teacher wrote down his name too and said firmly, "You are in, Ritesh. I am sure Abhay and Ritesh are going to make us all proud. You both can choose your topics. The contest is after four days."

Preparing For The Competition

The bell rang and the teacher left the class.

"This is all your fault," Abhay said angrily to Ritesh.

Ritesh too turned on Abhay, "Why did you **drag** me into this?"

Abhay shot back, "You dragged me first."

"I can't imagine **RECITING** a monologue in front of the whole school," Ritesh cried.

"You speak as though I was born for it. I can't **UTTER** a word in front of the teacher. What I would love to do to you," Abhay said controlling his fists.

Before Ritesh could reply, all the students surrounded them and started to **CONGRATULATE** them. This somehow had a good effect on the boys and they cheered up a bit.

Later at night, in bed, both were wondering what was going to happen on the day of the competition. Abhay wondered whether there were any chances of the competition being **CANCELLED** on account of heavy rain or some sort of a **strike**. Ritesh couldn't sleep and when he did, all he **dreamt** of was being on stage and repeating a single word again and again like a puppet.

A day before the competition, Abhay asked Ritesh **glumly**, "Are you ready for the monologue competition?"

Ritesh answered, "I have collected all the information on the topic I am going to speak about. I will **MEMORIZE** it later after school. What about you?"

Abhay said worriedly, "At least you have collected the information. I am yet to decide on a topic. Is there any topic on which I can speak in just one word?"

Ritesh said with a **mischievous** grin, "Yeah. The topic is you, yourself."

Abhay asked innocently, "Huh? Me?"

Ritesh laughed and said, "Yeah. You can speak about yourself in just one word. The word is DUMMY!" Saying this, he ran away quickly. Abhay ran after Ritesh hoping to catch him, but Ritesh was too fast for him.

Ritesh spent the entire night trying to MEMORIZE his speech. Meanwhile, Abhay had prayed that he would fall sick and not go to school.

On the day of the competition, the teacher came and spoke to the boys.

The teacher said, "Hope you boys are ready for the big moment. Which one of you boys is going to win the award?"

Both gave her a phoney smile. The teacher wished them luck and went away.

Stage Fright And Wit

The boys stood near the stage and waited for their names to be called. Abhay muttered, "Hopefully, they will forget to take my name."

Ritesh teased, "If they forget, I will REMIND them."

Then, Ritesh stuck his tongue out at Abhay, and the latter made a face at him.

As the minutes lapsed, both grew nervous and fidgety. By the time Abhay's name was called; his hands had become very damp, and his mouth very dry.

Abhay proceeded to the stage with his heart beating fast. He took his place on the stage. There was PIN-DROP silence all around.

All of a sudden, Abhay was looking at the whole school and they were looking at him. His mind went blank. He didn't know what to say.

All the students were looking at Abhay in ANTICIPATION.

Abhay knew he had to say something. Unfortunately, he forgot the topic itself. The students became RESTLESS because of the silence.

The students yelled, "Say something!"

Abhay had had enough. He quickly walked OFFSTAGE.

Next, Ritesh's name was announced. He went on stage and stood directly under the spotlight, smiling confidently at the crowd.

Just when everyone thought Ritesh was going to start his monologue, he too waved at the audience and walked away.

Their teacher met Abhay and Ritesh offstage. Both looked very **UNCOMFORTABLE** and avoided looking at each other.

The teacher asked them in **DISBELIEF**, "What had happened to you both? Were you not prepared? Why didn't you both say something?"

Abhay put on a **phoney** smile and said, "Ma'am, actually my monologue was about how to remain quiet against all odds which I **demonstrated** effectively."

Not to be outdone, Ritesh said, "And Ma'am, I didn't say anything because, in a monologue, a person goes on speaking till the others pull their hair out in **BOREDOM**. I didn't want the student body and the teachers to become **bald**. So, I sacrificed the award for their sake."

The teacher was shocked by their replies.

As she walked away, she thought to herself, *Maybe I should be the one to receive the award for* **CHOOSING** *them.*

Rain of Stars!

By Satish Roy

Every morning, Eddie the Donkey and his friends Rocky the Dog and Harry the Horse would have **TEA** at Rio the Bear's shop. One such morning, Eddie picked up a **newspaper** and started reading it.

"Oh no! We are in grave **DANGER**!" Eddie exclaimed.

"What do you mean, Eddie?" asked Rocky, a little alarmed.

"The newspaper says that stars are going to fall on Earth tonight! There is going to be a **SHOWER** of stars! If you don't believe me, here, read it yourself," said Eddie worriedly.

"A shower of stars? What is that? I have only heard of **RAIN** showers," said Harry, confused.

"A star shower means that stars will **fall** from the sky and **burn** everything on Earth," explained Eddie.

"What do we do now?" asked Rocky, scared.

Looking For Safety

"There is only one way out. We will have to hide at a **safe** place before it gets dark," said Eddie. He then asked Rio to shut his shop and go along with them.

"Once the stars fall on Earth, it wouldn't be safe for you to stay outside," he cautioned.

Rio agreed. And the four now ran *FRANTICALLY* looking for a safe place.

Trump the Elephant, who saw them running, asked, "Where are you all off to? And why do you look **FRIGHTENED**?

More Animals Join In

"Don't you know? The newspaper said that there was going to be a shower of stars tonight. We are all in danger," said Eddie.

Now, Trump was also **SCARED** and started running along with them in search of a safe place. Along the way, many others also joined them.

When they reached the school, the school teacher, Charlie the Rabbit, stopped them and asked, "Why are you all running? Is something wrong?"

"Yes! We have to find a safe place to stay before it gets **dark**," said a visibly tensed Eddie.

"But what is the problem?" asked Charlie **CURIOUSLY**.

A Logical Explanation

Eddie POINTED to the newspaper and said, "Read here. It says that there's going to be a shower of stars tonight."

Charlie then read the newspaper and looked at them with a SMIRK. "Oh! So all of you are panicking because of this piece of news?" asked Charlie, amused.

"Why are you smiling?" asked Harry, baffled at Charlie's behaviour.

"There will be a shower of stars, but there is nothing to WORRY about. Nobody is going to be hurt," said Charlie.

"How come? Won't the stars hit Earth and burn everything?" asked Rocky.

"No. Come inside and I shall explain everything," said Charlie, leading them to the classroom.

"What the newspaper is referring to is a **meteor SHOWER**," said Charlie.

"What is a meteor shower?" one of them asked.

"Meteors are basically small pieces of rocks floating in outer space. When they enter the Earth's atmosphere, they melt, leaving behind a trail of dust and other gases that make them look like objects on fire," explained Charlie.

"So, they won't burn Earth?" asked Trump.

"No, and if the sky is clear at night, it looks **beautiful**. We can see the meteor shower

with our naked eyes," replied Charlie.

Everybody heaved a sigh of relief.

"Thank you for clearing up our **CONFUSION**, Charlie. We **blindly** believed what Eddie said and started running behind him," said Harry.

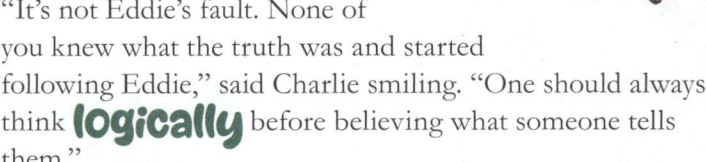

"It's not Eddie's fault. None of you knew what the truth was and started following Eddie," said Charlie smiling. "One should always think **logically** before believing what someone tells them."

Solve It

In an underwater neighbourhood, there are three schools of fish that feed off the same field of seaweed. There is always just enough seaweed for all the fish, not more and not less—and every night the same amount grows back.

The school of whales has 7 members, the school of manta rays has 6 members, and the school of small fish has 16 members. In one day, if one whale can eat 5 stalks of seaweed, a manta ray eats 1 stalk of seaweed, and a small fish can eat 1/4 of a stalk of seaweed, how much seaweed grows in this underwater neighbourhood?

Hesitation No More

By Harish Bhandari

Manu was a quiet and **Shy** girl. She spoke very little and was never involved in any fights at school or home. She did not even fight with her little brother Aditya, who would trouble her whenever he had the chance.

His school teachers would **COMPLAIN** about him at every parent–teacher meeting.

But Aditya was a bright student and good at sports, just like Manu, who had recently been selected to play **volleyball** for her school team at the national level. Her team even won the first prize in the competition held in Odisha.

No Questions

Manu was so shy that she never asked any questions in class even when she had a **DOUBT**. Her classmates had named her the 'shy girl'.

Manu's parents were worried about her shy and hesitant nature. Her father was an army officer. Manu's behaviour **worried** him, but he knew it was a trait that she had inherited from him. He, too, had been shy as a boy, but eventually, he had opened up and mingled with everyone.

But Manu did not change even after primary school, and her mother started worrying.

Manu's classmate, Diya's mother once told Manu's mother, "It is not good for anyone to be so shy and hesitant. It gives other children a chance to **tease** her, as they know she won't say anything in return. I suggest you speak to her."

"I have spoken to Manu. She likes being on her own and I don't want to force her to change. All kids have their **personalities**. I am always there to guide her," replied Manu's mother.

It's not that Manu was not smart. She was very good at her studies and all the teachers knew that.

Her friends, Teena, Riya and Varnika, never paid **attention** to what the teachers were saying. Instead, they spent time **IMITATING** their teachers and having fun. Whenever a teacher wrote a question on the **blackboard**, these girls made paper tails and stick them to the backs of the students who would get up to answer the question. This would make the entire class **LAUGH**. While Manu did not like their behaviour, she could not complain because she was hesitant.

Manu In Trouble?

One day, Manu's mother met Riya and Varnika in a market. She asked them how Manu was in class, thinking they were her friends and would thus know about her. The two girls instead took this chance to get Manu into **TROUBLE**.

"Aunty, Manu doesn't pay attention in class, and when the teacher asks a question, she just starts crying," Varnika said.

"She never finishes her classwork. That's why she always gets a C grade," added Riya.

To that, Varnika made another remark, "She's always scared!"

Manu's mother realised what the girls were up to. She understood that it was time Manu spoke for herself. She went home and told her husband what the girls said. They both knew that Manu was good at studies and always completed her classwork.

Encouraging Manu

Manu's father called out to her. He told her what her friends had said about her doing badly in class.

Getting no reaction from her, he said, "Manu, your friends have just said bad things about you and you have nothing to say. Does that mean it's true?" Manu nodded.

"Manu, you are a good girl. It's okay to be shy, but it is also necessary to talk if something wrong is happening. You should STAND UP for yourself."

Manu was quiet and sad. She thought Riya and Varnika were her friends. Her father knew she was upset.

He continued, "You don't have to be scared to speak the TRUTH. You have the biggest treasure in your hand. Your books! Remember, books are a student's best friend, as they show them the right path. You spend a lot of time with books

and have learnt so much. Then, why hesitate when you have so much KNOWLEDGE?"

Manu listened to her father carefully. She said, "Papa, from now on, I will try to participate more in class. I will also correct my friends when I think they are wrong. I will not shy away from standing up for myself."

Manu's new-found confidence made her parents happy, and they HUGGED her tightly.

And They Became Friends

By Richa Chhapolika

Rohan and Meera were close friends. One day, when Meera saw Rohan sitting on the school grounds looking glum, she asked what was bothering him.

"I am upset with how Shashi and his friends have been behaving. They are always troubling other children. Today, they tore Gautam's diary. I saw everything and yet I could not do anything about it," Rohan said sadly.

"Oh! So, this is the reason. You know they cannot be reformed. Why are you spoiling your mood by thinking about them?" said Meera, trying to cheer him up.

Rohan agreed with her and shifted to the subject of their discussion to exam preparation.

The Essay Announcement

The next day, the principal circulated a notice to all the classes, announcing that students who wrote a good essay on the topic "Our Camp" would be appointed as volunteers at the summer camp. Three students had to be selected from each class.

All the children were very excited and quickly got down to writing the essay. However, Shashi, as usual, started DISTURBING other students and would not let anyone write their essays.

"If you keep troubling us like this, I will COMPLAIN about you to the principal. He is very strict and he will expel you from the camp," Rohan said.

Shashi stared angrily at Rohan and reluctantly sat down in his seat.

MEERA'S MISSING ESSAY

Meanwhile, Meera had gone to the washroom and when she returned she saw that the paper on which she had been writing her essay was not on her desk.

"Where is my essay?" Meera screamed. She looked for it

everywhere. Hearing the **COMMOTION**, their teacher entered the classroom.

"Sir, Shashi has stolen Meera's essay," said Sonia. All the students joined her in **BLAMING** Shashi as he was the one who was always making trouble.

The teacher angrily said, "Shashi! I have been getting complaints about you for a long time. **Stealing** is not a good behaviour. As a result, I am **EXPELLING** you from the essay-writing competition, and you will not be allowed to attend the camp."

Rohan Defends Shashi

To everyone's surprise, Rohan came to Shashi's defence.

"Sir, Shashi has not stolen Meera's essay. I was watching Shashi all the time so that he does not trouble anyone and hence I can say that Shashi did not steal the essay," Rohan explained.

The teacher announced that he would check everyone's bag to solve the mystery of the missing essay. Each student was asked to step out of the classroom for the **SEARCH** to begin.

While the teacher was saying this, Sonia quietly tore Meera's essay and put **PIECES** of the paper in Shashi's bag.

During the search, as **suspected**, the essay papers

were found in Shashi's bag. He was called inside to give an explanation.

"Now tell us, Shashi, do you still want us to believe you did not steal the essay? These were found in your bag," the teacher said, showing Shashi the torn PIECES.

The Truth Is Revealed

Once again Rohan defended Shashi, "Sir, I have proof that Shashi is not the thief but Sonia is," said Rohan.

"Sir! Sonia stole the essay and tore the paper to pieces. Then at the right moment, she shoved these bits of paper into Shashi's bag. She did it so that Shashi would get caught and she would not be suspected," continued Rohan.

"If Shashi had stolen the paper, how are the same bits of it in Sonia's bag," asked Rohan showing the bits of paper he found in Sonia's bag.

Sonia was asked to explain herself to everyone. She confessed that she was JEALOUS of Meera, and stealing her essay was the only way to stop her from volunteering for the camp. Since Shashi had a REPUTATION for being a troublemaker, it was easier to blame him.

The teacher expelled Sonia from participating in the essay-writing competition. Shashi thanked Rohan for his support and promised that from now onwards, he would mend his ways. After some time, Rohan and Shashi became good friends.

Spot the Difference

Circle 10 differences you can find between the two pictures.

Shantanu's Wild Adventure

By Inderjeet Kaushik

Shantanu and his classmates went on a school **trip** to a nearby forest. While on their way, the boys played games and sang **SONGS** on the bus.

No Smoking!

While driving, the bus driver pulled out a **CIGARETTE** and lit it. "Mr Driver, please stop smoking on the bus. The smoke is making us **COUGH**," said Shantanu to the driver.

His friends joined him, too: "See the sign over there. It says 'Smoking is **PROHIBITED** here.' Please put out your cigarette."

When more students began to complain, the driver had no choice but to **COMPLY**. After a while though, he began lighting another one. This time, the boys complained to their teacher who made sure that the driver didn't **SMOKE** in the bus again.

When they were almost halfway there, the driver stopped the bus to take a **BREAK**. When he got out to stretch his legs, Shantanu quickly pocketed the driver's **matchbox**, so that he wouldn't be able to smoke for the rest of the day.

Soon, the group reached the forest and while some kids played games, some decided to find a river or **LAKE** to bathe in. They asked Shantanu to join them, but he declined saying, "I'm afraid of water."

"Well then, **Mr Scaredy Cat**, stay here and take care of our things while we take a nice dip in the river," said the others and left Shantanu alone in the woods.

Although the forest was calm and Shantanu enjoyed the sounds of **nature**, he couldn't help feeling that he was being watched. Suddenly, a low, deep growl came from some nearby place. It caught Shantanu by surprise and his heart began **beating** fast. He thought it must be a leopard or panther crouching close to where he was.

Shantanu looked around and just as he had predicted, a black **PANTHER** emerged from the bushes. Its yellow eyes were fixed on him.

Quick Action

Shantanu tried to think of a way out and suddenly remembered that the panthers were scared of **FIRE**. Slowly, Shantanu pulled out the matchbox he had taken from the driver and lit a match. He reached down slowly and picked up a dry tree branch, and lit it. Soon, it was burning bright like a **TORCH**.

When the panther saw the fire, it **stopped** coming closer to him. As Shantanu moved towards it, the panther kept moving back. Eventually, the panther ran away when Shantanu doused the torch and heaved a sigh of RELIEF.

All his friends came running up to him. "You're so BRAVE, Shantanu," they said. "When we heard the panther's GROWL, we immediately got out of the water, but by the time we could come to you, it was already there. So we stayed quiet behind the bushes and watched you drive it away. We're so sorry for calling you a COWARD," said one of the boys.

"Don't worry about it. Let's enjoy our picnic," said Shantanu and they all went to join the rest of their class.

Achoo!

By Asha Sharma

At school, students teased Bani, calling her "ACHOORO" because she sneezed throughout the day. The moment Bani entered her class, someone whispered, "Achooro has arrived."

Bani heard the comment and looked down. She then hesitantly raised her eyes and felt as if every child in the class was looking and laughing only at her. She got nervous and took out her **handkerchief** from her skirt's pocket, clutched it tightly, rolling it in her hand.

No One Wants To Sit Near Bani

Walking slowly, she sat on her chair. As soon as she sat, Vinay, who was seated next to her, slid further AWAY.

Bani was feeling HORRIBLE. She looked at Vinay from the corner of her eyes, quietly opened her book and started reading it.

Then suddenly her nose started twitching and before she could even take out her handkerchief and place it on her nose,

she sneezed loudly, "Achoo!" spreading the **DROPLETS** all around. Vinay mischievously whispered, "Achooro."

He then changed his seat just before Miss Soumya, their science teacher, entered the class.

"Vinay, aren't you supposed to sit next to Bani? Why have you changed seats without **permission**? Go back to your seat," instructed Miss Soumya.

"Sorry, ma'am, but Bani has again caught a cold and is sneezing all the time. I don't want to catch an **infection** from her," explained Vinay, staring hard at Bani.

Bani wiped her nose with her handkerchief and started turning the pages of her book.

What Are Allergies?

Miss Soumya glanced at Bani who was looking very sad.

"Vinay, Bani does not have a regular cold. She suffers from an **allergy**, which is caused due to the change in the weather. Her parents explained that during the rainy season, dust, **carbon** and pollution particles cannot travel higher and they are stuck in the lower layer of

the **atmosphere**, because of which we come into contact more. **Hypersensitive** people like Bani get allergies from this. **PRECAUTIONS** are necessary, but

you don't need to avoid Bani or tease her," explained Miss Soumya.

Vinay nodded but didn't change his seat. Miss Soumya then started teaching.

While talking to the class, Miss Soumya kept a constant watch on Bani. She saw that she was continuously sneezing and had a **runny** nose. She was using her handkerchief to wipe her nose, and touched her nose and mouth very often, maybe because she was feeling too **UNCOMFORTABLE**.

After the class, Miss Soumya went to Bani and whispered, "Meet me during the lunch break." As instructed, Bani met Miss Soumya. She was still touching her nose and mouth frequently.

Miss Soumya's Advice

"Bani, are you taking the **MEDICATION** prescribed by the doctor?" Miss Soumya asked gently.

Bani nodded her head. Soon after, she covered her nose with her hand, sneezed loudly and wiped her nose with the handkerchief.

'That's good, but along with the medication, you need to change some of your **HABITS** too, Bani. You have to stop touching your face so often. This is because we touch many surfaces with our hands and when our hands

touch our face and nose, the **GERMS** on our hands enter our nose and mouth, which adds to your allergy. Wash your hands with soap and water frequently throughout the day. You can also wear a **MASK** to protect yourself and others," said Miss Soumya.

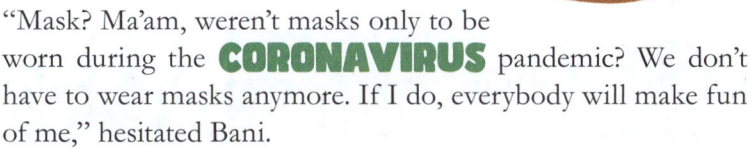

"Mask? Ma'am, weren't masks only to be worn during the **CORONAVIRUS** pandemic? We don't have to wear masks anymore. If I do, everybody will make fun of me," hesitated Bani.

Miss Soumya smiled and added, "During the coronavirus pandemic, we used masks to protect us from **VIRUSES**. But it is true that masks also protect us from small dust particles. Try wearing it and see if it helps you. And speaking of others making fun of you, we will talk about it in class. They will eventually stop **teasing** you," said Miss Soumya, lovingly.

Bani understood. The next day, she came to school wearing a mask. Everybody was smiling at her. She went and sat **confidently** in her seat.

Within a few days, her classmates realised that just by making a few changes in her habits, Bani's allergies had **decreased** to an extent. No one teased her anymore. Bani was happy she knew how to deal with her allergy in a better way.

Map Quest

Rehan had to meet his little sister Ayesha after school, but in this rain he can't find her among the other kids. Can you help him find her?
- Ayesha's favourite colour is yellow.
- Ayesha told Rehan that she would be waiting near the small fountain at the front gate of the school.
- Ayesha is always with her best friend, Sakshi, who rides a pink bicycle.

A Lesson in Equality

By Poonam Mehta

Mohit studied in the seventh standard at Golden Tulip School. The school also gave admission to some **bright** students whose parents were unable to **AFFORD** the school fees.

Rahul was one such student. Mohit, too, was bright, but he did not want to be friends with Rahul.

Mohit's Jealousy

"Why don't you want to be **friends** with Rahul?" Pulak, Rahul's friend, asked him during lunch break one day.

"What is your problem? Go and do your work," said Shivam, one of the boys in Mohit's group.

"I know the reason though. Before Rahul arrived, Mohit used to be getting the first position in class. But now Rahul is coming first, and that is why Mohit is **JEALOUS** of him," Pulak said.

""Run away, or I'll give you one tight slap!" said Shivam in a loud voice and **THREATENED** him.

"If Pulak thinks like this, then all the others must be thinking the same. Since Rahul has joined, all the teachers like him only," said Mohit after Pulak left.

"My grandma tells me that every person gets their chance to shine. Your day will also come," said Shivam, trying to **CONSOLE** Mohit.

The school bell rang and all the kids ran towards the classroom.

"Good afternoon, Sir," the students said collectively and stood up as the teacher entered.

The Sports Day Announcement

"Good afternoon students; sit down. I hope you all remember it is time for our Annual **Sports** Day. So, whoever wants to participate in the running event, please give me your names," announced the teacher.

All the students turned towards Mohit, as he was not only a bright student but also an excellent 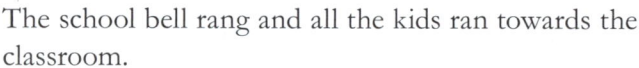.

"Okay, Mohit, I am writing down your name," said the teacher.

"Sir, I would also like to **PARTICIPATE** in the race," said Rahul and the entire class began to **whisper** amongst themselves.

"Yes, why not? I did not know that you are interested in sports," said the teacher and wrote down his name on the list.

After the teacher left, Mohit got very angry.

He went to Rahul and said, "You're definitely going to **LOSE** against me this time. I'm the best when it comes to sports."

Rahul smiled and kept quiet.

Mohit's Anger

Later that night, when Mohit and his family were having dinner, he said, "Father, I want the best sports shoes, as our Annual Sports Day is coming up."

"We got you new shoes just **TWO** months back. Why do you need a new pair?" asked Mohit's mother.

"No, they are worn out. I want a **NEW PAIR** that is the best one. There is a boy named Rahul in my class. He comes first in the class and I want to defeat him at least in this race," said Mohit angrily.

"Don't get so **ANGRY** while you are eating. Let's talk about it later. Finish your dinner first," said Mohit's father.

After dinner, his father took him to the study and asked him to sit down.

"Now tell me what is the matter?" asked Mohit's father.

"Since Rahul has joined the school, I have started coming second in the class. Now he wants to participate in sports events, too. I am getting very upset about this," said Mohit.

"Mohit, you must not compare yourself with anyone. It is not good for your mental well-being. You must embrace the challenge and work harder. You should compete with yourself to get better," Mohit's father tried to explain.

But Mohit was adamant about winning against Rahul.

The Race Begins

The next day at school, some of the students saw Rahul running practice laps on the track.

"I think he will win the race," said one of the students.

"That's only possible if Mohit allows it," said someone, and everybody laughed.

On sports day, all the students gathered in the school grounds. Rahul and Mohit were in the same RACE.

The coach blew the whistle and asked the students to take their positions on the running track.

Mohit glanced at his expensive new shoes, then looked at Rahul's relatively cheaper canvas shoes and smiled to himself.

The coach flagged off the race and all the participants sprinted.

For a few minutes, Mohit was ahead, but Rahul caught up with him and then overtook Mohit. Rahul won the gold medal and Mohit had to settle for silver.

"Sorry, you came second," said Rahul, consoling Mohit.

Mohit said, "That is okay. I was weighing success and FAILURE in the wrong way. My father was right. It's not status that makes us win, but hard work that pays. I should be the one to apologize." They hugged each other and soon became best friends.

We Are Equal

By Satish Roy

The primary school in Shanthivan decided to **implement** the midday meal plan.

The school principal Jumbo the Elephant announced, "Children, from tomorrow onwards, you will get **MIDDAY** meals in school. All of you can eat here. You don't need to bring food from home."

The Delicious Meal

The next day, when the lunch bell rang, all the children came to the lunch hall and sat down to eat. Jumbo and the teachers served the different varieties of **DISHES** prepared for the children.

"Wow! It's so tasty!" exclaimed Tinu the Rabbit.

"If we get good food like this every day, we will start loving school too," joked Mintu the Monkey as he gulped down a bowl of **KHEER**.

"Of course, the food will be **TASTY**. Hiroo the Horse has prepared it himself," said Jumbo, smiling.

But something happened the next day. The children looked sad. When the lunch bell rang, the children refused to come to the hall and announced that they would not eat.

Principal Jumbo was puzzled. He asked the students about the reason for their REFUSAL.

"Sir, we will not eat be able to eat the midday meal," said Tinu.

"But what is the reason?" asked Jumbo.

"We cannot eat the food cooked by Hiroo. If we eat it, then we all will fall ILL," replied Mintu.

A Shocking Reason

Jumbo was shocked. "What's wrong with Hiroo's cooking? He is a good cook. He washes all the vegetables before cooking and keeps the kitchen clean. I assure you that you will surely not fall ill by eating the food cooked by him," he explained.

"Sir, Hiroo is from a lower caste, whereas we hail from an upper caste. Our parents have told us not to eat the food cooked by him. We can eat only if the food is prepared by someone from the upper caste," said Tinu.

"So, this is the issue!" said Jumbo.

The next day, Jumbo invited all the parents for a meeting. He tried to reason with them that caste had nothing to do with food and falling ill. But the parents were not convinced.

"You cannot force our children to eat the food cooked by Hiroo. We will not allow it!" said Tinu's father angrily.

"But who believes in these things these days? People have reached the moon and here you are talking about CASTE," said Jumbo.

"Stop talking rubbish! Our children will not eat the food cooked by Hiroo. This is our final decision. If you force us, then we will stop sending our children to school from tomorrow," THREATENED Mintu's father.

Hiroo was upset. "Sir, if they do not want to eat the food cooked by me, then I will quit this job. I am the cause behind all these problems," said Hiroo to Jumbo.

"You don't have to go anywhere. It's not your FAULT," consoled Jumbo.

The King's Attitude

Amidst all the chaos, King Rana the Lion stopped by the school to pay a visit.

"Hiroo, I have come to eat the food cooked by you. I hear that it is very tasty," said King Rana, smiling.

All the students and especially their parents were SHOCKED. But Hiroo was scared.

"Maharaja, will you eat the food that I have cooked?" he asked **POLITELY**.

"Of course, that's why I am here. I am very **HUNGRY**. Bring me the food quickly," said King Rana. Hiroo served the food.

"Wow! I have not had such a delicious meal before. It really is tasty," said King Rana as he ate a mouthful.

Rana looked at the children and their parents, and said, "You can also sit with me and have this food."

"But Maharaja, if we eat Hiroo's food, our caste will be looked down upon. How will we answer our **community** members?" asked Mintu's father.

"Eating food cooked by another cannot be the reason for earning a bad name. I don't believe in caste or religion. Hiroo is no different from us; he is one of us. He is a member of our society and has as many rights and **privileges** as any of you do. We are all equal," explained King Rana. "When Principal Jumbo informed me about this incident this morning; I decided to come here in person and talk to you."

Regret And Food

Everyone hung their heads in **SHAME**. "Maharaja, we are ashamed of ourselves. We treated Hiroo unfairly. You have opened our eyes," said Tinu's father and pleaded for **FORGIVENESS**.

The other parents also apologized to King Rana and Principal Jumbo, and especially to Hiroo. They promised to never **discriminate** against anyone based on caste.

"Well done. I am glad that you have understood and changed for the better. The caste problem has plagued our society for many years, but now the time has come to remove this **EVIL**." said King Rana.

Everybody sat down with King Rana and **HEARTILY** enjoyed the meal cooked by Hiroo, who served food with a big smile on his face.

That's not right

Some things in this picture are not right. Find out what they are.

Seema Finds her Confidence

By Siddhesh Bhusane

Seema's family had recently shifted to Mumbai from a small town. In the new city, everything was new to her: the **WIDE** roads, tall buildings, **DOUBLE-DECKER** buses and shops the size of the local fairs back in her hometown. Even her school was going to be new.

Mixed Emotion

On the first day of school, Seema had mixed **emotions**—she was happy and worried. How is my new school going to be? How are my new friends going to be? Will they be nice to me? She wondered as she got ready for school.

After **BREAKFAST**, she and her mother left for school.

On reaching the school, Seema exclaimed, "Mummy, look how **BIG** the school is!"

"Yes, it is. And it is a good school. You should put in your best **EFFORT** to study and have some fun, too. Now, run along. I will come back in the evening to pick you up," her mother said.

Seema waved goodbye to her mother and proceeded towards her classroom.

A Bad First Day

As soon as she entered, the students in the class were curious to know about the plump, dark and **BESPECTACLED** girl as soon as she entered the classroom. She also wore two **well-oiled** braids. The kids found her amusing.

"She looks like she's come from a **village**. Wonder if she can speak English?" one of the students commented.

"Look at her glasses. They are so thick that they look like **binoculars**!" exclaimed another. All the students burst out laughing.

"And she has applied **TWO BOTTLES OF OIL** on her hair. Soon, oil will be scarce in our city," joked another student. Everyone laughed even more.

Seema felt sad. She sat alone on the first bench. The other students continued to make remarks.

The students became quiet upon seeing their class teacher enter the classroom. Anita noticed Seema on the front bench and said, "Hello! Aren't you the **new** student? What is your name?"

"My…n…name is S…S…S…Seema. Seema Kulkarni," she **stammered** in fear.

The students started laughing again.

"Quiet everyone!" Anita silenced the other students. She then turned to Seema and said warmly, "Welcome, Seema. Hope to see you do well in school."

Taunting Classmates

During the lunch break, many of the students from Seema's class went to the school canteen to buy lunch.

They bought pav bhaji, sandwiches, burgers, samosas and other tasty snacks, while Seema quietly ate roti and potato fry that her mother had packed for her.

"**ROTI AND POTATOES**! Do you think she knows what a pizza looks like?" one of the boys from her class asked his friend.

"They don't make pizzas in villages. She may know parathas!" responded the friend. The two laughed.

Seema felt like crying. She hoped for the day to end quickly. The **memories** of her old school kept her going through the day.

An Encouraging Shoulder

Finally, after what seemed like a long day, the last bell

rang. Seema rushed out of the school gate and into her mother's arms, crying.

"What happened, Seema? Why are you crying?" asked her mother, worried.

Seema told her mother about all the comments her classmates had made about her. "I don't want to go to this school anymore!" she cried.

"I understand how DEPRESSED such comments can make you feel. But you must not take them to your heart. Your classmates may not have interacted with anyone from outside the city. So give them some time and also the opportunity to learn who you really are—a talented, CHARMING girl who is liked by all her friends," her mother consoled her. "Anyway, I will also have a word with your teacher tomorrow."

Seema felt a little better after hearing her mother's words, but she still dreaded going back to school the next day.

Things didn't seem any different at school the next day or the day following that. Her classmates continued to pass COMMENTS about her and Seema sat quietly remembering her mother's words.

On the third day, during the school assembly, Anita went up on stage and said, "We will now have a special performance by a student. I hear she is a talented SINGER! I invite Seema Kulkarni on stage."

Seema froze on hearing her name. "What? Me? Sing?"

"Go on, village belle. You are Seema, aren't you? Or do you not understand English?" said one of her classmates, nudging her forward.

Talent Over Taunts

Seema walked up to the **STAGE** slowly. She could feel all the eyes on her. Anita handed over the microphone to her. "Go on, Seema. Show your classmates what you can do," she said, winking at her.

Seema closed her eyes and began to sing softly. Slowly, her confidence grew. Everyone was stunned to hear her sing, especially her classmates. After she finished singing, she received **thunderous** applause.

"I would like to thank my teacher, Anita ma'am, for **ENCOURAGING** me to sing and my classmates for this opportunity," said Seema.

Her classmates hung their heads in **SHAME**. The girl they had taunted for the past few days had thanked them in front of the entire school.

After the assembly, her classmates went up to her to **APOLOGIZE**.

"We are sorry for the way we treated you the past few days!" they said.

"That is okay. If it was not for your **TAUNTS**, our teacher wouldn't have asked me to sing in front of the school to help me increase my confidence," said Seema.

"And you sing very well! We had no idea you were so **talented!**" said one of her classmates.

"Will you be our lead singer for next month's inter-class music competition in school?" asked another student eagerly.

"Only if you will be my FRIEND," Seema said, smiling.

"Of course, we will!" said her classmates.

That day on, Seema found her CONFIDENCE and her friends learnt not to judge people by their looks.

Cheating the Teacher

By Padma Chaugaonkar

King Sher Singh's sons, Abhi and Rishi, ran up to him. They were **panting** and sat down to catch their **BREATH**.

The King asked, "What happened?"

Abhi replied, "We are very tired. We lost the game we were playing."

Sher Singh asked in surprise, "How did you lose the game?"

Lions Can't Climb Trees

Rishi replied, "Father, we were playing 'Catch me if you can' with Cheetu, Jeetu and Deepu. As we came close to catching them, they **climbed** up a tree! Since we didn't know how to climb a tree, they defeated us many times. We got **TIRED** trying to catch them."

"Children, this is our biggest **WEAKNESS**. We tried learning to climb trees, but it didn't work. Listen to this story," said Sher Sing and started narrating his tale.

"Long ago, tigers and lions were unaware of different **HUNTING** techniques. So, they would often have nothing to eat. Due to **STARVATION**, our species became physically weak.

"The cheetah, the leopard and the wild cat had a great reputation in the jungle. They were ***excellent*** hunters and **EXPERTS** in hunting techniques, like cornering, catching and

eating the prey. They were feared. These wild animals had claimed their right over a larger part of the jungle and had huge settlements.

Teaching Hunting Techniques

"One day, an old tiger thought, 'Let's send our children to the wild cats to learn the ART of hunting.'

"Everyone felt that if their children learnt hunting, they would never have to fear starvation.

"The lions and the tigers went to the wild cats with their request. They agreed to teach the children. However, they had a condition that they would only teach two students!

"The tigers and lions thought that this would be enough. In the future, those who have learned can come back and TRAIN the rest.

"A wild cat called Sonu was appointed as the teacher. Two bright and RESTLESS tiger cubs started training under him. Sonu trained them in different exercises, including bouncing, jumping and KNOCKING down each other. Sonu also introduced hunting techniques.

"The tiger cubs learnt skills like cornering the prey, NABBING and the proper use of claws and jaws. The

training made the tiger cubs skilled in many hunting techniques. They grew up to become FEARSOME hunters.

A Sudden Atack

"One day, during a practice session, the tiger cubs suddenly attacked Sonu. But Sonu was clever. She had already sensed their intentions from their attitude and gestures. As soon as the tigers rushed towards her, she quickly jumped back and climbed up a tree that was nearby.

"The tigers stared at her in surprise. They too, tried to climb but couldn't succeed. They asked Sonu in FRUSTRATION, 'Teacher Sonu, how come you didn't teach us how to climb a tree?'

"Sonu said, 'Dear students, we teachers give the most valuable knowledge only after testing and being sure about our students. Both of you felt that you had mastered everything. However, the one lesson that I had kept for the last saved my life. It's too bad that you didn't prove to be good students. If you had, you could have learnt this technique too. Go home now with whatever KNOWLEDGE you have grasped and never come back.'"

Jumpy's Pride

By Lalit Shaurya

Jumpy the Monkey was delighted. His examination results were out. He had passed with excellent marks and **TOPPED** his class.

He was excited to go to the next standard. He had already bought the new books.

"I am excited to go to the new class. It shall be loads of **FUN**," said Jumpy, excitedly.

"You are right, Jumpy. But we will have to even **STUDY** more than before," sighed Blacky the Bear, who was also being promoted to the new standard.

Jumpy's Overconfidence

Jumpy laughed and said, "Studying is a **piece of cake** for me. I'll do that easily. Didn't you see that I topped the class last time?" boasted Jumpy.

"But just because you topped the last time, it does not mean that you'll top the class this time, too. You will have

to study **harder,**" Blacky said.

"Don't you give me any advice! I know what I have to do," Jumpy **SNAPPED**.

"All right. From now onwards, I'll not tell you anything," Blacky said and left.

But Jumpy's focus on studies became **decreased**. He started spending more time playing.

He felt that being a topper in his previous class would automatically make him one in this class, too. He felt that he did not need to study as much.

"Jumpy, nowadays you're paying less **attention** to your studies. Playing is good, but, you should not keep on playing all the time. You will fall behind in your studies this way," said his mother.

"Don't worry, Ma. I'll top my class this time, too," Jumpy said confidently, not listening to her **advice**.

"Nobody can do well without hard work. You will have to study for that," his mother advised.

Jumpy got irritated and said, "We'll talk about this when

my exams come. Right now, I am going out to **play**."

Falling Behind

Slowly, Jumpy started falling behind in his studies. Soon, it was time for the unit tests. Because he had not put in the work, he got less marks and was very **DISAPPOINTED**.

"Jumpy, this time you've been very **CARELESS**. If this goes on, you will score low marks," his teacher, Cheeku the Rabbit, warned him.

"Sir, I'll be more careful next time. I'll pay more attention to my studies," Jumpy **promised**.

But after a few days, Jumpy forgot his priorities. He was once again not interested in anything but **playing**. Everybody tried to make him understand, but he was in his world.

"I will study during my half-yearly exams," he said to himself.

Slowly, the half-yearly exams drew nearer. Jumpy had not **PREPARED** anything. Now, it seemed difficult to even pass the subjects. He thought he would **CHEAT**.

An Awful Attempt

He made a few chits for his maths exam. But he was caught and taken to the principal, Jumbo the Elephant.

"Jumpy, what's this? You've been the topper in our school. How could you do this? You want to cheat and pass! I can **expel** you from the school for this," said Jumbo, sternly.

Hearing this, Jumpy started crying. Tears started flowing from his eyes. "I have made a grave **MISTAKE**, Sir. I will not do it again," cried Jumpy.

"Last year, you worked hard, so you topped the class. This time, you were careless and the result is in front of you. You cannot succeed without hard work. **OVERCONFIDENCE** is harmful. If you had studied every day, you would not have needed to cheat today," Jumbo explained.

"From today onwards, I will work hard. Please **forgive** me," Jumpy replied to Jumbo as he understood the importance of hard work.

"This must never happen again," Jumbo cautioned him and let him go.

Jumpy took his exams and came back home. On reaching home, he told everything to his mother and hugged her.

"It's okay now, Jumpy. Mistakes happen. We must learn from them. Success is not permanent. It depends on our **hard work**."

Jumpy made a study timetable and started working hard on his studies once again.

Back To School

Find as many words as you can related to school from the word search below.

Z	G	N	S	T	U	D	E	N	T	L	V	Q
P	D	O	S	A	Y	U	A	J	E	I	G	U
Y	E	T	E	L	X	A	O	Y	G	L	U	E
Q	J	E	C	L	U	B	O	O	K	S	E	F
W	U	B	E	E	J	N	S	T	G	H	R	R
R	U	O	R	T	E	A	C	H	E	R	A	K
I	R	O	X	J	I	X	T	H	Q	P	S	R
T	P	K	O	W	J	P	B	M	B	E	E	E
I	M	A	M	D	E	Z	H	U	D	O	R	L
N	A	L	P	N	I	G	Z	T	M	R	X	U
G	T	K	C	E	R	M	L	B	N	L	G	R
R	H	I	L	G	R	G	N	I	D	A	E	R
P	L	A	Y	G	R	O	U	N	D	R	E	I

Blinded by Pride

By Laifong Wong

Jay was an **INTROVERTED** child and thus had only a few friends. He thought that people would make fun of his low marks and that not many would want to be friends with him.

One day, the class teacher asked all the students to create something useful out of **WASTE** for an assignment and bring it to school the next day. Jay was excited because he wanted to use this opportunity to prove himself.

Jay's Brilliant Idea

The next day, Jay brought two old clay pots to school and explained how they could be used to make an innovative clay **REFRIGERATOR**. He demonstrated by placing the small clay pot inside the larger one and filling the gap between the two pots with **sand**. He then poured cold water over the sand.

"The wet sand will keep the food placed inside the smaller pot **FRESH**. This device can be used to store **LEFTOVER** food," he explained.

He also informed his teacher that he was planning to install a clay refrigerator in his neighbourhood, so that everyone could put leftover food in it, and the same could be DISTRIBUTED amongst the poor later.

The teacher was extremely impressed by Jay's idea and awarded him the highest score on the assignment. After that day, Jay realised that his strength lay in thinking CREATIVELY, and he began applying it in all his assignments. He slowly gained confidence, which was also reflected in his studies, as he began scoring well in all subjects.

Popularity And Pride

The following academic year, Jay was made the monitor of his class. He soon became a popular student at school, and everyone wanted to befriend him. But pride changed him—he insisted on his friends adhering to his "rules", failing which he would remove them from his group. Finally, his friends decided they had had enough of his behaviour and stopped talking to him.

Not having any friends made Jay sad and lonely again. He lost his confidence and kept to himself most of the time; he didn't talk much with his parents.

Then one day, Jay's father saw him frantically searching for something at home.

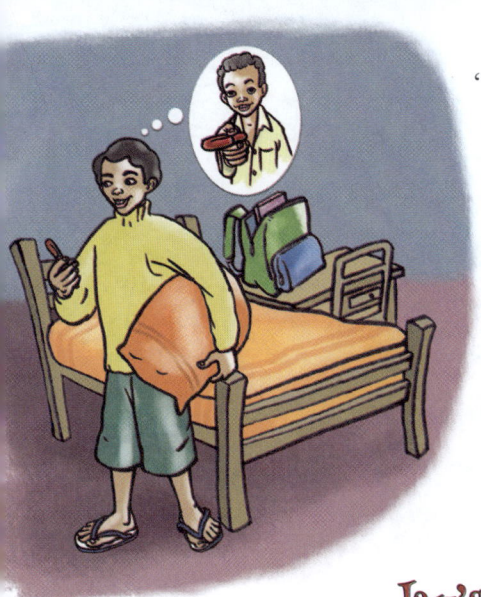

"What are you looking for?" asked his father.

Jay did not answer and continued looking for his **LUCKY** pen which he used for all his exams. It was a special gift from a friend. He looked for it everywhere—in school, the playground, his study table, but he still couldn't find it. He was **PANICKING**, as his exams were starting the next day.

Jay's Realization

When Jay returned from school the next day, his father asked him, "Did you find what you were looking for?" Jay did not answer this time either.

"Sometimes, the things we are looking for are right in front of us, but we **FAIL** to see them. Instead, we go looking for them outside," said his father, who had observed that Jay had not been his usual self at home.

Jay suddenly **REMEMBERED** using the pen to take some notes while studying the previous night. He searched his bed and finally found the pen under his **pillow**.

When he looked at the pen, he recalled the time when he was popular in school and how he started treating everyone **badly**, especially his best friend Sanjay, who had gifted him the pen on his birthday two years ago. Jay felt ashamed now. Pride had **BLINDED** him to his true friends.

Friendship Over Popularity

Jay ran crying to his father. Hugging him, he **confessed** his mistake. His father consoled him and told him that he had to apologize to his friends for his behaviour.

The next day at school, he saw Sanjay, who was sitting in the row next to him, **struggling** to write with a broken pen. This was his chance. He quickly offered Sanjay his lucky pen and **gestured** that he was sorry. Sanjay accepted the pen, with a smile on his face.

From there on, Jay did not aspire to be a popular kid in school. He just wanted to be a **good** friend.

In a New City

By Lalit Shaurya

Priyanshi was feeling both upset and NERVOUS. It was a new city, a new school and she didn't know what to expect.

Her father had been TRANSFERRED from Uttarakhand to Chennai. He worked for a bank. She had been admitted to a prestigious school in Chennai. There were only two days left for the school to open after the SUMMER holidays.

Priyanshi's Hesitation

"Mumma, I'm very SCARED. Who will I talk to? I don't even know the language spoken here. I speak Hindi. Everyone here speaks Tamil. There will be new faces all around. I don't feel like going to school," cried Priyanshi, tears welling up in her eyes.

"Don't worry, my dear! Everything will be fine. Slowly, you will make new **FRIENDS**. You will also learn a new language. You know English, right? You can talk to your friends in English, and gradually, you can teach them Hindi like they will teach you Tamil. Take one day at a time and we will see what happens," her mother **REASSURED** her.

Priyanshi gathered some courage from her mother's words. Two days later, when the school opened and Priyanshi went to school, everything was **NEW**.

However, she felt **relieved** when she was greeted with a smile by everyone she came across.

Making A New Friend

Priyanshi's eyes fell on a girl sitting silently in a corner. She **approached** her and said, "Hi, I am Priyanshi. What's your name?"

"My name is Shalini," the girl replied in Hindi.

Priyanshi jumped with joy upon hearing **Hindi**. She exclaimed, "You can talk in Hindi? Do you live here?"

"Yes, I can. I have recently joined this school. My father is in the **ARMY**, and he has been posted here in Chennai," replied Shalini.

"Oh, wow! Shake hands with me! From today, we are best friends! I'm

also new here. I've come from **Uttarakhand**," said Priyanshi, excitedly shaking Shalini's hands.

Priyanshi and Shalini developed a deep **friendship**. They started spending time together and had no problem at school anymore.

Overcoming Barriers

The two girls also became friends with a girl named Priya, who was a resident of Chennai. Priya spoke both **FLUENT** Tamil and English.

"Can you **teach** us how to write and speak in Tamil?" Priyanshi and Shalini asked Priya.

Priya agreed. She started teaching Tamil to them, while Priyanshi taught Priya how to speak Hindi.

After a few months, both Priyanshi and Shalini became **proficient** in Tamil. While Priyanshi started speaking Tamil fluently, Shalini became **SKILLED** at writing Tamil.

Meanwhile, Priya started speaking and writing in Hindi. She could enjoy listening to Hindi songs and even MEMORIZED many of them.

One day, there were announcements regarding various competitions in the school. Priyanshi participated in the speech competition, while Shalini took part in the essay-writing COMPETITION.

Priyanshi worked hard, practising for hours in front of the mirror. Priya also helped her. Shalini, on the other hand, prepared a good ESSAY.

A Life-Changing Competition

On the day of the competition, Priyanshi, Shalini and Priya were full of CONFIDENCE.

Priyanshi delivered a brilliant speech and Shalini wrote an IMPRESSIVE essay. Priya sang 'Vaishnav Jan To', Mahatma Gandhi's favourite bhajan, in Hindi at the beginning of the programme, earning PRAISE from everyone.

After some time, the results were announced. Priyanshi secured the first position in the speech competition, astonishing everyone with her fluent Tamil speech. Shalini received second place in the essay-writing competition.

All the children applauded enthusiastically. Priyanshi and Shalini attributed their **SUCCESS** to Priya.

Now, both the new city and language felt familiar to Priyanshi. She felt it had now become her second **HOME**.

Isha's First Day

By Dr Narendra Chaturvedi

When little Isha learnt that on the first day of the next month, she would start school, she was very happy. She jumped around the house, thinking about all the fun she was going to have there.

As the days went by, her parents started **BUYING** her all the things she would need for school. With just a day to go, Isha had everything she needed for her first day. She had a pretty little bag filled with **COLOURFUL** books and a new set of uniforms and shoes, too.

New Things For Isha

Her little brother, Chirag, looked at all her things in awe. He couldn't help but open her bag and see what was inside.

"Be careful," said Isha. "They're NEW."

"Sorry, I was just looking," said Chirag.

"All right, go ahead. But don't turn the pages. They might TEAR," said Isha.

"Is this your lunch box?" asked Chirag, picking up her casserole.

"Yes, that's a casserole. It will keep my lunch nice and warm," said Isha.

"Your shoes are so nice," said Chirag.

"Uh-huh," said Isha. "I have two pairs. One is to go with the regular uniform and one is for the sports uniform. On Saturday, I can wear whatever I want. I'll wear a new **FROCK** every week."

Chirag really wanted to go to **SCHOOL** too. But he'd have to wait another year before that happened.

In the evening, Isha's friends, Pinky and Shweta, came over to play. They were all going to board the school bus together the next morning.

"Will you come to see me off in the morning, Chirag?" Isha asked him.

Chirag nodded and resumed playing **FETCH** with Shweta's dog, Peter.

That night, Isha had packed all her **BOOKS** and readied her uniform for the next day. She could hardly wait. The next

morning, Isha's parents rode with her on the bus and took her to her classroom. They introduced her to her class teacher.

School Begins

Isha immediately took a liking to her new school and her TEACHER. She sat right next to her teacher who said sweetly to her, "You have such a nice name."

Isha smiled and said, "Thank you, Ma'am."

"You seem to have made a lot of friends today. Are you having FUN?" asked the teacher.

"Yes, Ma'am, I am," said Isha.

"Very good," said the teacher. "Do you have any friends outside school?" asked the teacher.

"Yes, I do. Shweta and Pinky are my BEST friends. They are older than me, but we play together every evening," said Isha.

"That's nice," said the teacher. "How many people are there in your family at home?"

"There's me, Chirag and my parents," said Isha.

"Is Chirag your brother?" asked the teacher.

"Yes, he is. He's younger than me, but he's my best friend too," said Isha.

"That's great," said the teacher. "Why don't you stay here? I'll be back in a minute," she said and stepped outside.

The Theft

As Isha sat in her place near the teacher's desk, she saw that a strange man was peeping inside through the window. Isha felt nervous. After looking around, the man climbed in through the window and walked towards the teacher's bag.

Isha immediately ran to the teacher's chair and **GRABBED** the bag.

"Who are you? Go away!" she said to the strange man. But he didn't listen to her and tried to snatch the bag.

Isha held on **TIGHT** and refused to let go. She called out to her parents, who were outside, paying Isha's fees. The thief **YANKED** hard on the bag and knocked Isha down. She burst into tears and **cried** out loud.

Hearing her cries, her parents came running. Startled, the **THIEF** jumped out of the window and escaped.

When her parents came, they asked her what had happened. Hearing all the commotion, the teacher understood that Isha had foiled a theft attempt. She took her bag from Isha and hugged her.

"Isha, you've not even finished your first day and you've already done a great thing," said the teacher. "I had my money, my phone and my credit cards in that purse. Thank you for not letting that man steal my purse," said the teacher.

Isha knew she would enjoy her time at school.

 Memory

Observe the picture for a minute, cover it and try answering the questions given in the box.

Q1. What does the circular signboard say?
Q2. How many children are waiting with their parents?
Q3. How many buses are there on the road?
Q4. Is the dog running ahead on the leash?
Q5. What is the name of the tea stall?

Mittu Goes To School

By Rohini Chintha

Mittu did not like going to school. He found it boring and **TIRESOME**. He was always making up excuses to **skip** school. He pretended to have a tummy ache or headache, and sometimes he even **refused** to get out of bed. Even when he was up, he complained and cried and mumbled.

Mittu's Unexpected Holiday

Mittu's mother was tired of his **antics** every morning. She wanted Mittu to love school and agree to go by himself and not by force.

So, one day, Mom decided not to wake up Mittu for school. The alarm buzzed, but Mittu **pretended** to be asleep. His mother watched him but said nothing. Mittu was glad. After a while, his mother got ready, said bye to Mittu and left for her office. Mittu could not believe what was happening! Mom didn't even ask him about school. He wondered whether it was a **HOLIDAY** at school for some reason.

So after Mom left, Mittu called up his classmate Sunny. But Sunny had already gone to school. Mittu was thrilled about

the **UNEXPECTED** holiday. He jumped and danced and played all day. He watched TV for hours.

When his mother came back in the evening, Mittu expected her to scold him for wasting his time. Instead, she pleasantly greeted Mittu and went on with her work. Mittu was even more **SURPRISED** now.

Freedom From School

This went on for two more days and the **PRINCIPAL** of the school called. Mittu's mother just said that Mittu was fine and would attend school after some time. But Mittu resolved never to go to school again. He kept his books away and watched TV and *played* all day.

But then, after a couple of weeks, Mittu got bored of watching TV all day and playing alone. He wanted to talk to his friends, but they were at school in the morning and were busy with **HOMEWORK** in the evening. He **MISSED** all the fun times he would have with them. He missed his favourite teacher,

Miss Rose. He felt like doing something in his spare time but as he had no homework, he was **bored** in the evening, too.

Mittu's Return

He was now tired of staying at home. He **FEARED** that his mother would never send him back to school. Then he would know nothing about the world, remain in the same class forever, and have no friends and future.

This thought frightened Mittu so much that the next morning, as soon as the alarm buzzed, Mittu got up, got ready, had breakfast and rushed off to school. In the evening, he sat down to finish all the **PENDING** work. He studied hard every day after that and started **LOVING** going to school.

His marks improved and his teachers were happy with him. His mother was very happy to see this change in Mittu. Most of all, she was happy that Mittu had realised the **IMPORTANCE** of going to school, without her **PUNISHING** or scolding him. Now the morning time in the house was the most pleasant time of all!

The Wrong Kind of Help

By Vinay Bharat

There were two best friends—Aahnvi and Shanvi. The little girls studied together in Class 1. Bright-eyed Aahnvi EXCELLED in her studies, and the creative Shanvi loved to paint but did not care much about her studies.

One day, their class teacher Ms Soreng, conducted a QUIZ. "Can anyone name the different colours of the RAINBOW?" asked the teacher.

Aahnvi quickly raised her hand. "Violet, indigo, blue, GREEN, yellow, orange and red!" she answered.

"That's right Aahnvi! Come up to the front, please," said Ms Soreng. The class clapped. The teacher congratulated Aahnvi for answering **correctly** and hugged the little girl.

Shanvi Sulks

Now, Shanvi, who was watching all of this, felt JEALOUS. When Aahnvi returned to her seat, she saw Shanvi SULKING. This puzzled Aahnvi.

"What is the matter, Shanvi?" she asked.

"I will not SHARE my lunch with you from now on," said Shanvi, tearing up. "Nobody loves me. Not even you!" she SOBBED.

Surprised, Aahnvi exclaimed, "That's not true. You are my **best** friend!"

But Shanvi continued to cry.

"Don't be sad! Please don't cry or else I too will," pleaded Aahnvi, now in **tears**.

However, Shanvi ignored her **plea**. "It's true! Why else would you not share your answers with me during the exam?" said Shanvi, crying.

A Silly Arrangement

Aahnvi understood why Shanvi was upset. "Very well!" she agreed. "This time, I will share all my answers with you. That is a promise. Now, please **cheer** up!" smiled Aahnvi.

Shanvi stopped crying. The girls looked at each other's **tear-stained faces** and giggled. All was well again with the two best friends.

Now, the second term exams were fast approaching.

This time, Aahnvi put in a lot of effort in preparing for the **exams**. Her mother, Reeta, was happy to see her daughter work **HARD**. Little did she know that Aahnvi's extra effort

was because she had promised to help Shanvi in the upcoming exams.

The exact opposite happened at Shanvi's home. Relaxed, Shanvi did not bother studying for the exams. Her mother, Geeta, was worried about her daughter's *careless* approach to her exams.

On The Day Of The Exam

The day of the examination arrived. Both the girls reached the exam hall.

Ms Soreng handed out the question paper. As soon as Aahnvi saw it, she was *thrilled*! She knew all the answers. Happily, she quickly began writing down her answers. But she had promised Shanvi that she would help her, and Shanvi was a *slow* writer. Soon, Shanvi kept interrupting Aahnvi, asking her to slow down, as she found it hard to write quickly.

The *final* bell rang. The first exam was over. All the students submitted their answer sheets. Since Aahnvi had to slow down to let Shanvi copy from her answer sheets, she lost out on *PRECIOUS* time. The hardworking girl could not complete her exam, leaving it two answers short.

Feeling *TERRIBLE*, Aahnvi cried. She went home, feeling sad. Meanwhile,

Shanvi was happy! She had managed to copy all of Aahnvi's answers and was sure of getting a good rank.

Finally, the results were declared. Both their mothers, Reeta and Geeta, were called to **COLLECT** their respective report cards.

The Parents Intervene

Reeta was surprised to learn that her daughter Aahnvi, a **topper**, could only secure the third rank. Meanwhile, Geeta was surprised that her daughter, Shanvi, despite not putting in any **effort**, shared the third rank with Aahnvi.

The mothers, who were also good neighbours, chatted. They soon realised what had happened. They called Aahnvi aside. She was crying because of her results. With a little **COAXING**, she shared the entire incident.

Geeta called her daughter over. "Apologize to Aahnvi. What you did was wrong!" she said. She then turned to teary-eyed Aahnvi, "My child, never do that again. **CHEATING** is a crime, and to let another cheat is also a crime. Your actions, instead of making her successful, will set her up for **FAILURE** in life. She will never know her weakness and will never work hard to **IMPROVE** it. This sort of blind love will make her

dependent on others for life. It will handicap her. If you really love your friend, share your books, knowledge, everything, but, before the examination. Be firm in life, Aahnvi, and do not sway from the **RIGHT** path," Geeta advised.

Reeta, who was listening to all of this, had tears in her eyes.

The little girls realised their mistakes. They **HUGGED** each other. And from then on, both Aahnvi and Shanvi started studying hard, together.

A Piece of Paper

By Omprakash Kshatriya

Riya and Shraddha walked out of the examination hall together.

Riya asked, "You seemed very **NERVOUS** during the exam today. What was the matter?"

"I was scared when I saw a piece of paper," replied Shraddha.

Riya asked, "Which piece of paper are you talking about?"

The Suspicious Piece Of Paper

"Look! The exam was going on, and someone threw it at me. Do you remember I wrote some **NOTES** on a similar piece

of paper while we were coming to **school**? I used it for revising on the way."

"Yes," said Riya, "And...?"

"I was scared to see it near my table. What if the **invigilator** saw it, too? She could have thought I was cheating!"

"Yes, and...?"

"When you **panic**, your brain stops working. So, I took a deep breath to calm myself. I figured it was better to tell the teacher that a piece of paper was lying there. But then I thought—what if the paper contains my **handwriting**?

"That's when a voice came to my mind: *What could happen, after all? The teacher would scold me and say that I'd brought the paper to* **copy** *from it. Then I would have to* **deny** *it and say that I didn't bring it,*" said Shraddha. "So, I called the teacher."

Telling The Teacher

"The teacher asked, 'Yes, Shraddha?'"

"There's a piece of paper lying there," I said.

"'Where did it come from?'" she asked.

"I don't know, Ma'am! Someone **threw** it there," I said.

She picked up the piece of paper and started reading it. Then she looked at my answer sheet and asked, "Aren't you appearing for your English exam today?"

"Yes Ma'am!" I replied.

"'This has maths notes on it,'" she said, throwing it into the bin. And I heaved a sigh of relief.

Accepting One's Mistake

"But I still don't understand who could have thrown the paper at my desk," wondered Shraddha.

Riya LOWERED her face and said, "It was me!"

Shraddha said, "So you brought it to CHEAT during the exam?"

"No," Riya said, "It was stuck in the crack of my table when I was taking the exam. I was horrified when I saw it. What if the teacher saw it and thought I was cheating? I would have been in trouble. That's why I quickly took it out from the crack and threw it away."

"And you had to throw it towards my desk!" Shraddha exclaimed.

"No, no!" said Riya. "I was throwing it the other way, but my hand hit the table, and it flew towards your desk. Please FORGIVE me. It was my mistake."

"But you could have just told the teacher!" Shraddha said.

"I was scared at that moment and couldn't think of anything else," Riya admitted.

Understanding Riya's situation, Shraddha said, "Oh! You were just as scared as I was."

"Yes, totally!"

"But why were we scared?" Shraddha asked. "We hadn't made any MISTAKE, so we shouldn't have been scared."

"You're right," Riya said. "We get unnecessarily ANXIOUS during exams and it also affects our PERFORMANCE."

"Exactly!" said Shraddha. "Let's try not to be unnecessarily scared during exams again."

"Agreed!" said Riya.

And together, they left for their homes, walking arm in arm.

PUZZLE TIME

Best Test

This story has been written with words and pictures. Can you read it?

Ronit and Suma went to the same 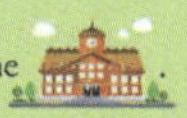.

Their class had a big 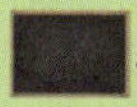.

One day, the 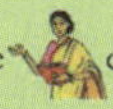 decided to take a test.

She read out a passage from a 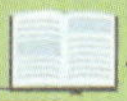.

They wrote it down in their 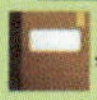, as she read.

Ronit's 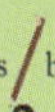 broke. He took one from Suma's 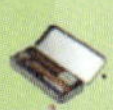.

The 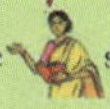 scolded him and gave him a new .

Later, they both scored 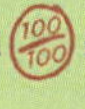 in their test.

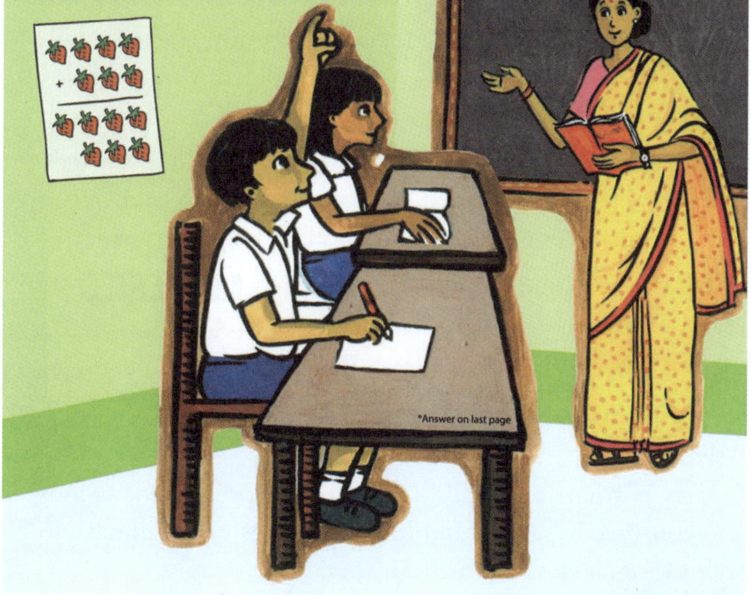
Classroom Test
*Answer on last page

The Forest Echoes with News

By Shiv Mohan Yadav

Leo the Lamb was **WEAK** in studies. His mother had arranged for a tutor, Harry the Hippo, to help him study after school.

Leo however, did not like going for **TUITIONS**. As usual, his mother pushed him to go to Harry's.

He pleaded, "Mom, please don't send me to Harry's classes. He beats me!"

"Leo, don't make up stories. If you don't study, Harry is going to be **CROSS** with you. Now, go!" scolded Mother, pointing towards the open door.

A scared Leo quietly picked up his books and started for Harry's place. He returned an hour and a half later. His eyes were swollen from **CRYING** and he looked very sad.

"Leo, why do you pretend as if Harry has **ILL-TREATED** you?" asked Mother.

"But mother, believe me! Harry **BEATS** me! I do not want to go to him again. Please, find me another teacher," said Leo, irritated.

"Harry is smart and well-known in the forest. Leo, as long as you continue to fall behind in your studies, you will have to go to him for classes," warned Mother.

Leo felt **helpless** as his mother refused to believe him. The little lamb stood in a corner, **SOBBING**.

The next day, Leo was watching television. His mother came in and snatched the **remote** from him. She then got him ready for classes. All the while Leo **pleaded**, "Please don't send me to Harry's. My back still aches from yesterday's beating."

He held on to his mother and would not leave her. She freed herself from his hug, "Leave now! Or else I will take you there myself!" she said, angrily.

Helpless Leo Finds Help

Teary-eyed, Leo made his way to Harry's place but found it difficult to go on. He stopped under the shade of a tree.

Suddenly, a car drove up and halted near him. The door opened and out stepped an antelope, dressed in a smart suit. He had a pair of **SUNGLASSES** on. He startled Leo.

"Son, why are you standing here alone?" asked the antelope, taking off his sunglasses.

Leo suddenly realised that he knew the antelope! He quickly **WIPED** his tears.

"Uncle Bobo!" cried Leo.

Surprised, the antelope, Uncle Bobo, asked, "How do you know me?"

"You are a senior **REPORTER** on the Jungle News channel, aren't you? I often see you on television," replied Leo.

"That's right," said Uncle Bobo. He looked sad. "But now I have been **fired** from my job," he said.

"Why? You are such a good reporter!" said Leo.

"My boss asks me to get interesting and **EXCITING** stories," replied Uncle Bobo.

"Oh!" said Leo.

"But, tell me little lamb, why were you crying?" asked Uncle Bobo as he looked concerned.

"My tuition teacher, Harry, beats me. I have told my mother this but she **REFUSES** to believe me. Instead, she **SCOLDS** me and sends me back to him. I am afraid he will beat me again!" said Leo, between sobs.

The Plan

"Well, son, don't cry. I will **accompany** you to Harry's home," said Uncle Bobo.

"He will not beat me in front of you, Uncle Bobo. But he will make up for it after you leave," said Leo.

"Then, I will hide and catch him **red-handed**," said Uncle Bobo.

"But, I will still get a beating!" said a scared Leo.

"No. As soon as he starts, I will **INTERRUPT** and stop him," explained Uncle Bobo.

"Ok," said Leo. "Please stop him **QUICKLY**."

"Go ahead," said Uncle Bobo. "I will follow you." With that, Leo started for Harry's place.

As soon as they reached Harry's house, Uncle Bobo **HID** behind the door. He took out his **video camera** and began recording all that was happening.

Suddenly, a loud voice **BOOMED** from within. "Why are you late?" shouted Harry.

Leo shivered and replied in a meek voice, "I met my uncle on my way here."

"You met your uncle, is it?" mocked Harry. "Do not waste my time! Show me your **homework**!"

Leo handed over his book to his teacher. "What a **TERRIBLE** handwriting! Why can't you learn to write neatly?" shouted Harry.

Uncle Bobo heard two loud **whacks** of the ruler, followed by a sob. Leo cried, "Please don't beat me! I promise to write neatly next time!"

Harry, however, was in no mood to be kind. He began to **pull** Leo's ear. Poor Leo howled, "Save me! Please!"

Meanwhile, Uncle Bobo was recording the video clip. As soon as he saw that Harry showed no signs of **stopping**, he quickly ran in.

The Truth Is Revealed

"Stop!" shouted an angry Uncle Bobo. Surprised, Harry stopped. Leo ran to Uncle Bobo and held him **TIGHT**.

Harry composed himself and said, "He never completes his homework, so I try to **FRIGHTEN** him. His mother tells me to be strict with him."

"You can harm a child with this cruel behaviour!" said a stern Uncle Bobo. Harry did not say a word.

Uncle Bobo walked out with Leo. He said, "Come, Leo, he will be **punished** for what he has done."

Soon, all the news channels in the forest flashed a **NEWS** story: "Teacher beats a young student!"

Leo And Bobo Find Happiness

Leo's mother, who watched Harry ill-treating Leo in the video clip on one of the news channels, could not believe her eyes. She felt terrible for not believing Leo. Just then, Uncle Bobo walked in with Leo, and his mother **EMBRACED** him.

Uncle Bobo said, "You should have listened to Leo when he tried to tell you about Harry's behaviour. If, like you, I too would have **FAILED** to listen to his pleas, he would continue to suffer Harry's cruelty."

Mother hung her head in shame. Soon, television channels were running another news story: "Harry is arrested."

Just then, Uncle Bobo received a phone call, "Congratulations Bobo! Welcome back on board!" said his boss.

Now, both Uncle Bobo and Leo's problems were **SOLVED**. They both looked at each other and smiled.

My Dearest Teachers

By Niloy Kurmi

Aruhi's face radiated with **excitement** when she came back from school. Papa found her smiling to herself and even humming a tune while she freshened up.

*I wonder why she is so happy today, he thought in the kitchen. These last few days, she has been very **GLOOMY** about having to change homes so suddenly.*

"Have you made new **FRIENDS** at school, dear?" Papa asked, putting a spoonful of rice on her plate. "See, I told you it was only a matter of time before you would."

A New Start For Aruhi

It had only been a week since they had moved to this town due to Ma's work transfer.

Aruhi had thrown quite a **FIT** about it. "I d-don't want to live h-here! I don't know anyone! I-I h-hate this p-place!" she had cried. But it had all been in **VAIN**.

She had even **refused** to go to her new school. "W-Why can't I be h-home s-schooled like before?" she'd demanded.

It took a lot of **persuasion** from Papa and Aita—her grandmother—to convince her to get ready for school on the **first** day. As Aruhi always listened to her mother, it would have been helpful if Ma had been there then, but she'd had to go to the office early in the morning.

Now, Aita asked Aruhi at the dining table, "Won't you tell us what was so special that happened in school today?"

"Teachers' Day is c-coming, you see, Aita," Aruhi answered, beaming ear to ear. "And g-guess what? As part of the c-c-celebrations, the students will organise a c-cultural FUNCTION at school. I'm thinking of p-p-participating!"

She leapt out of her chair and, twirling around the room like a TORNADO, exclaimed, "I shall dance!"

Then, she stood on the chair, and, while posing as a monarch holding a sword, said, "Or should I do d-drama?"

And then, holding a spoon like a MICROPHONE, she squealed, "Or I could even sing! How w-wonderful, right?!"

Both Aita and Papa calmed her down and asked her to finish her meal first. After that, she retired to her room. "I'm going to p-practise, as there will be a-auditions. Only the b-best p-participants will be selected," she explained. "So, please do not disturb me."

But the real reason Aruhi was so excited about the Teachers' Day celebrations were DIFFERENT.

If I can showcase my skills there, everyone will admire me, she thought. They will think I'm cool. They'll want to be friends

*with me. My teachers will be very **impressed** too!* And thus, daydreaming, she danced on her bed.

Aruhi's Disappointment

The next day, Papa and Aita were expecting Aruhi to return home in the same jolly mood. But alas, her face was etched with utter **DEJECTION**! She refused to speak to them and confined herself to her room all day.

She only opened her **heart** to Ma at night when she returned from work.

"I-I was d-d-**DISQUALIFIED** in the a-auditions, Ma," Aruhi sobbed, hugging her mother tight. "Some s-senior s-s-students laughed at my d-dance moves. T-they won't even l-let me sing!"

Ma tried to **CONSOLE** Aruhi as she wept in her lap. Aruhi wished they were back in their previous home. She wouldn't have to worry about going to school.

Rewinding Time

She missed her home tutor, Geetanjali Ma'am, who was her favourite teacher. Geetanjali Ma'am was always **PATIENT** with her. She understood her well. She was not like the new schoolteachers who always seemed to be in a rush.

Last Teachers' Day, Aruhi made a card for Geetanjali Ma'am with a little help from her father, who was a **CARTOONIST**.

She had also given Ma'am a bouquet of flowers she and Aita had grown in their garden.

This time, however, she hardly knew any teacher at school. Her classmates did not speak to her—and she felt all **ALONE**.

So, when she **DECLARED** that she wouldn't be going to school on Teachers' Day, no one could change her mind.

"Maybe you should call Geetanjali Ma'am," suggested Ma, hoping it would brighten Aruhi up.

But, on Sunday, everyone was worried again.

"What's she doing in her room?" wondered Aita, Ma and Papa, who were trying to **eavesdrop** outside Aruhi's door.

"Is she alright? Should we take her to the park? She's been in there all day!"

Nevertheless, they soon found out what Aruhi had been up to. The next day, 5 September, when Ma, Papa and Aita woke up, Aruhi handed each of them a card.

A Grand Gesture

"H-Happy Teachers' Day to all of you!" she beamed and **HUGGED** them. "After all, parents are our f-first teachers!" And indeed, that's what Geetanjali Ma'am had told Aruhi over the phone the other day.

Until now, Aruhi had taken for granted those teachers who guided her outside her classrooms. In this case, it was her parents—her **DEAREST** teachers of all.

Ma had taught Aruhi to dance and to be hardworking and **DILIGENT** in whatever she did. Papa had taught her drawing and painting. And Aita had taught her singing and **GARDENING**.

"I see you are getting ready for school," Papa pointed out later. "I thought you weren't going today."

"Gee-Geetanjali Ma'am t-told me it would be wrong if I d-didn't wish my t-teachers at school," Aruhi replied with a smile. "So, I've m-made **CARDS** for them too."

"Yes, that would be lovely of you," Papa smiled back.

A Box of Chocolates

By Nishi Patel

The hot summer breeze was starting to cool. Anjali was having some warm **IDLI** for breakfast with her Grandma, when she said, "I wish every morning would be just like this!"

"My dear, enjoy till it lasts," said Grandma.

A Bitter Realisation

Anjali thought about what grandma meant, and soon she realised that school **VACATIONS** were over and she would have to rejoin school after the weekend.

"Vacations are **OVER**! I do not want to return to school anymore," said Anjali, bitterly.

"I thought you enjoyed going to **SCHOOL**, Anjali. You loved playing with your friend Aditya, didn't you?" asked Grandma, confused.

"Nani, he is changing schools as his family is shifting to Pune. Now, I don't like my school, as it won't be **FUN** anymore. I had only one friend and he has left," she cried.

As their breakfast was over, Grandma didn't say anything and wondered how she could **cheer** up Anjali.

Nothing Can Stay The Same

The afternoon was Anjali's favourite time of the day as she would watch the afternoon light brighten her room.

"How **pretty** the sky looks!" exclaimed Grandma, walking inside Anjali's room. But Anjali did not respond as she was busy wondering how she could ever go back to school.

"Nani, can I just never go to school?" she asked, **WISTFULLY**.

Grandma asked, "Why, my dear?"

"Because school will never be the same again!" said Anjali.

Though her grandma knew the **reason**, she still wanted to confirm it. "Is it because Aditya will not be coming to school anymore?" she asked, softly.

"Yes, Nani!" agreed Anjali.

"Oh! How many students are there in your class?" asked her grandma.

"There are 40 students. Why?" wondered Anjali.

"Wow! So many! Well, then you can make a new friend," suggested Grandma.

Finding Happiness

Anjali thought for a moment and sighed. She replied, "But they will not be the **same** as Aditya."

Then Grandma suddenly got up and came back with a box of **CHOCOLATES**.

"Here, have some!" she said, offering the box to Anjali.

"Wow! So many different types of chocolates. I would like to have this…" Anjali thought about which to pick.

"Today is World Chocolate Day!" winked Grandma.

"So, July 7 is celebrated as World Chocolate Day! Amazing! I had no idea, Nani!" exclaimed Anjali, as she picked one and started nibbling on it.

"Can I have one more?" she asked.

"What if the other chocolate does not taste as good as the first one?" asked Grandma.

Anjali laughed as she found the question silly. She said "What? Not at all. It is okay to at least try and taste it!"

"That's true!" agreed Grandma and asked, "Did you like any new ones?"

"Yes! I think I found my new favourite," replied Anjali, pointing to the one she was eating.

Chocolates And Classroom

Grandma smiled and said, "Well, so you see, trying out different chocolates is not a bad idea."

"Of course, it's not."

"Well, my dear, don't you think a CLASSROOM is like a chocolate box? Try talking to different students. Who knows you could make a new friend!" continued Grandma.

Anjali's eyes widened in surprise. She loved the idea of a classroom being like a chocolate box!

"Nani, that's amazing!" said Anjali, "I never thought of it like this. I cannot wait to go to school now!"

Hearing that, both of them chuckled.

"What does that mean?" asked her brother, Arjun, walking into the room.

Anjali and her grandma explained everything that had happened.

Arjun asked Anjali, "So, you are not sad anymore about missing your old friend, Aditya?"

Anjali sighed and replied, "I am sad and I will miss him, but that does not mean that I should not talk to my other classmates. I mean, who knows, I might make a NEW friend."

"Yes, that is a good idea, Didi!" agreed Arjun.

The next day, Anjali felt NERVOUS and excited at the idea of talking to different classmates. She waved goodbye to her grandma and went to school with a spring in her step.

Hidden Picture

Can you find the musical instruments hidden in this scene?

First Day at School

By Ashima Kaushik

Jojo and Mojo, the tiger **twins**, were starting their first day at school. Jojo was scared while Mojo was excited.

They had new bags, water bottles and lunch boxes, and were also wearing new shoes. Mojo loved his new shoes, but Jojo was scared of the **squeaky** noise his new shoes were making.

Roma the Camel, Jojo's friend who also went to the same school, tried to cheer Jojo up: "It is just a **playschool** and will be a lot of fun!" They walked to the mango tree and stopped.

A Long Wait

"Let's wait for the others to join and then we all will walk to the school together."

"Is it FAR?" asked Mojo.

"Nah, it's just round the corner," replied Roma playing with her new YO-YO.

Soon, Shona the Sheep, Coco the Cat and Donna the Duck joined them.

"Let's go," said Donna, marching ahead.

"We need to wait for Toto. He should be here any minute," said Shona. They saw Toto the Turtle TROTTING at his pace.

"He is always so slow. We are all going to get late because of him," complained Coco.

Suddenly, they heard a loud thud. It was Wimpy the Hippo. "Get out of my way," HUSTLED Wimpy as he passed by Toto and pushed him off the track. Toto almost fell into a pit, losing his balance but his shell saved him.

Mojo growled at Wimpy. Nobody had ever GROWLED at him. Meanwhile, Jojo scuttled behind Roma.

"Be quiet," hushed Shona.

But it was too late. Wimpy turned around and yelled, "Who growled?"

"No one," said Shona, Coco and Donna quickly.

"Move everyone, we can't be late for the first day of school. Let's go!" said Roma, DISTRACTING everyone.

First Day Nerves

On reaching the school, Roma made sure Jojo and Mojo found their **classroom**, as it was their first day at the playschool.

Jojo hesitated at the door, looking **PALE** but Mojo ran to take the first seat in the classroom.

"Come in," yelled Mojo. "Look, there are so many **TOYS** here!"

Jojo slowly came and sat next to Mojo. He felt like **CRYING**. But Mojo was already playing with the wooden train set, which distracted Jojo.

Soon, Miss Rita the Deer came. Seeing her, Roma ran to her classroom.

Miss Rita greeted everyone with a big **smile** and gave **snack packs** to each of them. Mojo quickly opened his and ate everything. Jojo saved his snack pack to eat later.

Miss Rita then handed sheets of paper with a picture of a tree on each to all the kids. She gave **CRAYONS** in a cup for everyone to share and colour the pictures.

Mojo quickly picked up a red crayon, started **scribbling** on his sheet and was soon done with the colouring exercise. He went back to play with the toys.

Jojo slowly completed colouring his tree, using green and yellow crayons. Miss Rita gave him one more snack pack as a reward for the best colouring.

Then, it was time for a story. All the students **laughed** and enjoyed as Miss Rita narrated a funny story. During lunchtime,

everyone went outside to play. Mojo ran to the **swings** and Jojo followed him. Both had a good time.

The Day Ends With A Punch

At the end of the day, Roma came to get Jojo and Mojo. And they all walked back with Shona, Coco, Toto and Donna.

Mojo excitedly told them about the fun he had with the toys and swings at school. Jojo took out one of the snack packs that Miss Rita had given him.

He was about to open the packet when Wimpy passed by, and SNATCHED the packet from his hand and said, "Come and get it!"

This was **enough** for Mojo. He couldn't tolerate his twin being bullied. He charged and growled at Wimpy, "Give me the packet right away!"

Wimpy laughed and taunted Mojo, "Oh really!" and **opened** the packet.

All the animals were **scared**, while Roma was quiet and Toto hid inside his shell.

Mojo punched Wimpy on his nose and that started a big **FIGHT**.

During the ongoing chaos, Toto, who was inside his shell till now, walked close to Wimpy and tripped him. Wimpy fell on his face and everyone's mouth opened in **SURPRISE**. Mojo climbed on Wimpy, snatched the packet and walked away. He handed over the packet to Jojo.

Mojo felt like a hero. He and his group of friends felt that **together** they could do anything. They couldn't wait for the second day of school!

School Search

PUZZLE TIME

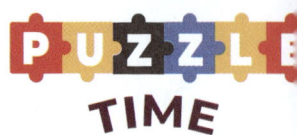

It's Rohan's first day of school after summer vacations, but he can't remember the way! Can you help him find his way?

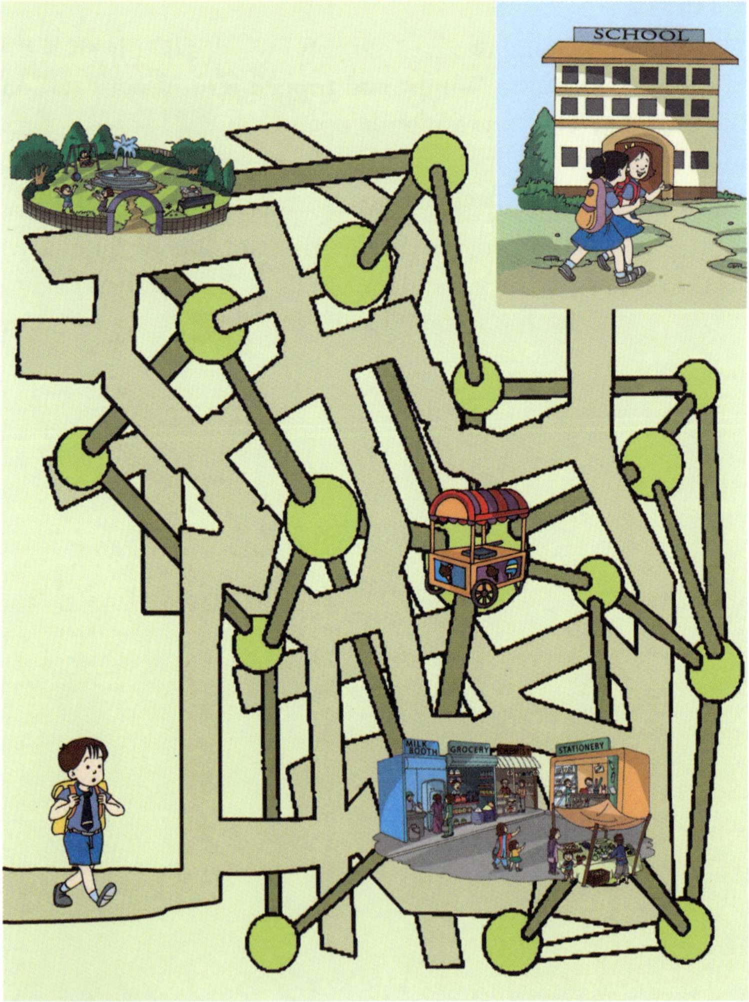

Answer

PAGE 123: HIDDEN PICTURE

PAGE 131: SCHOOL SEARCH

PAGE 78: BACK TO SCHOOL

Z	G	N	S	T	U	D	E	N	T	L	V	Q
P	D	O	S	A	Y	U	A	J	E	I	G	U
Y	E	T	E	L	X	A	O	Y	G	L	U	E
Q	J	E	C	L	U	B	O	O	K	S	E	F
W	U	B	E	E	J	N	S	T	G	H	R	R
R	U	O	R	T	E	A	C	H	E	R	A	K
I	R	O	X	J	I	X	T	H	Q	P	S	R
T	P	K	O	W	J	P	B	M	B	E	E	E
I	M	A	M	D	E	Z	H	U	D	O	R	L
N	A	L	P	N	I	G	Z	T	M	R	X	U
G	T	K	C	E	R	M	L	B	N	L	G	R
R	H	I	L	G	R	G	N	I	D	A	E	R
P	L	A	Y	G	R	O	U	N	D	R	E	I

PAGE 36: SOLVE IT

Whales eat - 7 X 5 = 35 stalks
Manta Rays eat - 6 X 1 = 6 stalks
Small fish eat - 16 X 1/4 = 4 stalks
Total - 45 stalks of seaweed grows there everyday.

PAGE 15: SOLVE IT

1. Today was the first day of school. I got dressed quickly and ran all the way there, where I met Meeku and Jumbo. I climbed up on Jumbo to see if we would all be in the same class.

2. Yes! Meeku, Jumbo and I were together. Our first subject was History and we went to class.

3. After attendance was taken, our teacher wanted to know what we did in our vacations. When it was my turn, I told the teacher how I learned to swim.

4. After school, I said bye to my friends and returned home.

More in the Series

Join Kalpana Chawla on her voyage into space; cheer for Slurpy the stray pup as he defeats Darwin's theory; be with Jay when he gets his Polio vaccine, and catch Linu the honeybee experimenting with nanotechnology. Try to find the weight of a donkey without using a scale, and solve the mystery of the disappearing lemonade with Jumpy the monkey.

Go on a thrilling journey with this must-have collection that encourages thinking and is filled with humour and adventure!

Champak Science Stories makes science fun and easy—the way it should be